# PERFECT MATCH: CAPTAIN'S CONQUEST

## PERFECT MATCH SERIES

### I. T. LUCAS

# GREGG

"The usual?" Gregg's favorite Starbucks barista smiled.

It wasn't the rehearsed customer service kind, but a genuine smile reserved for friends. Or so he hoped.

"You know it. Any new sandwiches on the menu?"

He couldn't care less, but that would get her talking, and he loved the sound of her voice.

"Nothing new. But I recommend the cheese and basil."

"Then that's what I'll have."

"Toasted?"

"Naturally."

She took the sandwich out, put it in a paper bag, and wrote his name on it. "That would be ten fifty-two."

He gave her a twenty. "Keep the change."

Holding the bill, Alicia narrowed her eyes at him. "That's too much." She put it into the register and handed him back a five. "For your next coffee."

He knew better than to argue with her. "How about I buy you one?"

She laughed. "Coffee? I don't drink the stuff."

"You work here, and you don't drink coffee?"

"If I did, I couldn't sleep."

"How about decaf?"

She shook her head and then glanced at the next customer in line, letting Gregg know that his time was up.

"Oh well. Thanks for the sandwich suggestion."

"You're welcome. See you later, Gregg."

And that was it. He'd been coming there for months, sometimes twice a day, sometimes three times, and the frequency had nothing to do with Starbucks' mediocre coffee and everything to do with Alicia.

Why hadn't he asked her out yet, then?

Because she wasn't his type.

Gregg didn't date tattooed and pierced rocker chicks. Hell, he didn't date at all if he could avoid it. His mother kept trying to set him up with her country club friends' female progeny, and sometimes he had to humor her and agree to a date.

But other than that, he was perfectly satisfied with casual hookups.

He wasn't looking for a relationship, especially not with any of those spoiled rich girls who bored him to death. And if he brought home someone like Alicia, his mother's fragile heart would fail on the spot. He loved his mom too much to risk that.

Besides, it wasn't as if he wanted a relationship with Alicia either.

She fascinated him, and he would have loved getting to know her intimately, but, unfortunately, she didn't seem interested.

"A double espresso and a toasted sandwich for Gregg!" the guy behind the counter called out.

Taking his order to a table with a good view of his girl, Gregg sat down and spent the next twenty minutes pretending to read on his phone while observing Alicia from the corner of his eye.

If he could only find a way to hook up with her, he could finally get her out of his system and stop wasting time at Starbucks.

His partner was on his case about that, and although Gregg's money, or rather his parents' money, had been the seed investment that had funded their company, he still needed to put in the work.

While Sam handled the business side, Gregg was the technical brain and in charge of their cybersecurity operations. If any of the programmers needed assistance, he was the one they turned to.

There was only so much he could accomplish while loitering in a coffee shop and ogling a girl he shouldn't.

Except, he couldn't stay away, and Alicia wasn't responding to the subtle hints he was throwing around. Today was as close as he'd ever gotten to asking her out, but her response or lack thereof had been pretty clear. She wasn't interested.

Would she change her mind if she found out how rich he was? Or if he lost the baggy shorts and flip flops and put on something that made him look good?

Gregg didn't want to do either. She either liked him for who he was or not at all. The world was full of gold diggers and airheads who were impressed by fashionable clothing, and he wanted nothing to do with those types, not even for hookups.

They tended to be as boring in bed as they were to talk to.

Was he jaded?

Kind of. Probably.

His mother was worried that he would never marry because he was too picky, and there was some truth in it. At thirty-four, he'd been with a lot of women, and none had captured his interest beyond a second date.

Which probably meant that the problem was his and not theirs.

Except, if wanting a woman that he could have an intelligent conversation with and share a laugh with was being too picky, then so be it. He wasn't willing to compromise on that.

Besides, he was spoiled by the virtual world of the Perfect Match studios. He hadn't found his true love in there like his partner had, but he'd enjoyed many satisfying virtual sex adventures, and he couldn't care less what the women behind the gorgeous avatars looked like in real life.

He enjoyed the fantasy. Hell, he was probably addicted to it.

"I knew I'd find you here." Sam clapped him on the back. "You have a serious coffee addiction, buddy." His partner pulled out a chair and sat across from him. "I just came back from a meeting with the Perfect Match board of directors. They are opening three more locations, and naturally they hired us to handle their cybersecurity."

"That's great. I'm glad Hunter and Gabriel are doing so well. A year ago, they were still paying us with gift certificates."

Sam chuckled. "We can sell them. They are worth a lot of money today."

"I'm sure you are going to keep a few for you and Lisa. Don't you want to go back and relive the fantasy?"

Lisa had been working in the same office building as them for years, but until she and Sam had been matched by pure chance in the virtual world of Perfect Match, they had never even spoken to each other.

Uncomfortable, Sam straightened his tie. "We've only done it that one time. Real life is better than fantasy."

"I'm sure it is."

Maybe it was for Sam and Lisa, but not for Gregg. He would take fantasy over reality any day.

Except, glancing at Alicia, Gregg's conviction wavered, but only for a moment. What if instead of lusting after a woman he couldn't have, he created a virtual fantasy with someone like her?

He could design his next adventure with his tattooed barista in mind.

If he described her in detail on his request form, the program would create a lookalike avatar for him. He could then pretend he was playing with Alicia and not some random woman using that avatar.

Or he could do better than that.

What if he could find out what Alicia's fantasy was, give her a gift certificate, and then design his fantasy to match hers?

He knew how the algorithm worked, and if he collected enough pointers from her wish list, he could fill in his questionnaire in a way that would ensure them getting matched.

That was the perfect solution.

Why hadn't he thought of that sooner?

He could have his cake and eat it too.

Was it a bit dishonest?

Probably. But Gregg could live with that.

2

## ALICIA

*W*hen Alicia was sure Gregg wasn't looking, she snuck a quick glance at him, admiring his chiseled jaw, his broad shoulders, and the corded muscles that were visible under his worn-out T-shirt.

Who did he think he was fooling with those hobo outfits he wore?

Not her, that was for sure.

Everything other than his clothes indicated that Gregg was far from poor. His perfect haircut was not the kind one got at Supercuts, and his wallet, which had seen better days, had at one time cost several hundred. From her short stint working in Nordstrom men's department, Alicia recognized the brand at a glance.

But the most telling was the company he kept.

She could hear snippets of conversation between him and the guy in the tailored suit who'd joined him. It seemed that the two were partners in a cybersecurity company, and they had just scored a big new contract.

Why was Gregg hiding behind schlumpy outfits?

Did he want to slum with the plebs?

Perhaps he was one of those guys who was paranoid about getting caught by gold diggers and wanted to hide the fact that he had money.

Or maybe he simply liked well-worn clothes that were loose and comfortable. Her younger brother was like that. Jeff couldn't stand wearing anything even slightly rough or scratchy, and he always cut out the tags because they irritated his skin.

Still, if Gregg had asked her out, she might have gone out with him despite his idiosyncrasies. But he had never gone beyond friendly flirting, and she assumed he was taken. Which might explain his wardrobe choices. Perhaps the baggy shorts and flip flops served as a shield against unwanted advances.

There was no ring on his finger, but that didn't mean a thing. If Gregg was sensitive to scratchy fabrics, the same might be true of jewelry.

Besides, she didn't have time for dating. Between her day job and her band practices and occasional gigs, Alicia always felt rushed.

"The guy is too good-looking for his own good," Marcy said when there was a lull in the line of customers.

"Which one?"

"Don't pretend like you don't know. You should ask him out."

"Me? I'm not going to ask a guy out."

"Why not?"

"Because he might say no."

Marcy waved a dismissive hand. "So what? You just move on to the next one. Men do it all the time."

"Well, not me."

Shaking her head, Marcy leaned against the counter. "With those tattoos and piercings, you look like a tough rocker chick, but that's just war paint, isn't it?"

Alicia smiled but didn't answer, saved by a customer with a prepackaged salad approaching the counter.

"Would that be all, sir?"

"I would also like two grande double mocha cappuccinos, please." The guy whipped out his wallet.

Marcy wasn't wrong. In fact, she'd nailed it.

Alicia was a great singer. She had an impressive vocal range and a notebook full of original songs that she'd written. But image and looks were just as important for success in the music world. And the don't-mess-with-me look served her well when performing in nightclubs.

Most of the time she managed to fake the appropriate attitude as well, but it wasn't easy.

Alicia could cuss with the best of them, but it was like spitting nails. And she could act mean when necessary but would then feel awful about it.

The real Alicia was a geek, an obsessed *Star Trek* fan, including all of its spinoffs and sequels, loved watching *Doctor Who* on BBC and was as adventurous as a school librarian.

In fact, Ms. Adams, her old high school librarian, was probably much more daring than her. Those thick glasses of hers hadn't been able to hide the mischievous-bordering-on-evil spark in her eyes, and there had been rumors of her having an affair with the very married gym teacher.

Go figure.

"Goodbye, Alicia." Gregg waved at her from the door. "I might stop by later today, and if not, see you tomorrow."

"Bye." She smiled and waved back, hoping he would return.

Even if nothing ever came out of his flirting, she was always looking forward to his visits.

They were the highlight of her day.

## 3

# GREGG

*B*y the time Gregg was finished at work, Alicia's shift was over, and there was no point in going back to Starbucks.

Sam had already gone home to his family, which left the option of hanging out with the staff at the local bar. But that always felt awkward. They played along and pretended that Gregg was one of the guys, but they weren't having as much fun with him around.

Except, he didn't want to go home either. His next virtual hookup was scheduled a week from now, and he wasn't in the mood for bar hopping.

Pulling his top desk drawer open, Gregg looked at his stash of Perfect Match gift certificates, picked up one of the blue envelopes, and put it on top of his keyboard.

How was he going to do it?

It wasn't as if he could stand at Alicia's counter and spend an hour interrogating her about her hobbies and interests. He could perhaps sneak a question here and there, but now that the idea had sprouted, he was too impatient for collecting information one piece at a time.

Except, the girl had turned down his subtle invitation to coffee, so it wasn't as if she was going to suddenly accept an invitation for a date.

Perhaps there was somewhere he could corner her?

But where?

He didn't even know her last name. But that was easily fixed. After all, he was a cybersecurity expert, and there was no shortage of hackers among his staff.

He picked up the phone and dialed Drake's extension. The guy usually stayed after hours, racking up overtime which Gregg was happy to pay.

"What's up, boss?"

"I need a favor. You know the Starbucks around the corner?"

"What about it?"

"A barista named Alicia. Can you hack into their HR and find out her last name and age?"

If she was under twenty-one, it was a no go.

"No problem. Do you want her address and social as well?"

It was tempting, but Gregg preferred to look her up on social media and find out stuff she was sharing publicly. Anything else would be too creepy.

"No, that would do."

"I'm not going to ask why you need it."

"Good." Gregg hung up.

Less than ten minutes later, his phone rang.

"Alicia Beatrice Fraser, age twenty-six."

"Thanks."

Gregg thought she was younger. Twenty-six was good.

"You're welcome."

Now that he was equipped with her full name, it was a piece of cake to find her on social media sites, and she was on each one he could think of.

Apparently, Alicia was a singer, and she was doing her

damnedest to promote herself and her band via every channel possible.

The best part was finding out that she was performing tonight, and that he still had time to get to the club.

Gregg smiled. *Game on, Alicia.*

4

# ALICIA

"*How* ow does it look?" Alicia asked.

Peeking from behind the curtain, Becca scanned the club and shook her head. "Not much of a turnout tonight."

"It's fucking Wednesday," Peter said. "That's the worst day of the week. That's why we got it."

Alicia sighed. People thought that being in a band was all that, but the reality was far from glamorous for most musicians, even the good ones.

It wasn't enough that they weren't paid, they also had to buy stage time by selling tickets to their own show for the club. And if they didn't sell enough, they weren't going up. Which meant that the four of them had been hustling like crazy to make the cut.

"Look on the bright side," Becca said. "At least we get to go in front of an audience. That's better than most bands get."

Grumbling about how sucky his life was, Peter hooked up his bass to the amplifier. Raven, who hardly ever said anything, shrugged her slim shoulders and got behind the drums.

"Ready?" Becca lifted her guitar.

12

"Shouldn't we wait for a signal?" Alicia glanced at the back door, looking for the club owner.

"He said to start at eight o'clock sharp."

"Okay, then." Alicia took her spot behind the microphone.

As soon as Becca started her intro, the curtains parted, and Alicia switched to performer mode. It was like an alternate self emerged whenever she was on stage.

"Welcome, everyone, and thank you for coming. We are the Stargazers. Becca on lead Guitar." She waited for the applause. "Peter on bass." More clapping. "And Raven on drums."

Raven did a quick solo that got her another round.

"Give it up for Alicia, our fabulous lead singer!" Becca introduced her.

With lights shining into her eyes, Alicia couldn't see how many people were on the dance floor, but she could estimate by the sounds of clapping. The place wasn't full, but it wasn't a bad turnout either.

As long as she got to sing in front of an audience, she was good.

# 5

# GREGG

*a* bottle of beer in hand, Gregg leaned against the back wall and waited for the curtains to lift, which was a nice prop, but unusual for a dance club. Usually, the DJ or the band just went on and started playing.

The place wasn't packed, but there was no seating inside the club. The entire interior was occupied by the bar and the dance floor, and the only seating was outside. A large covered patio provided tables and chairs, and smoking was allowed, which was a rarity these days.

Gregg wasn't a smoker, so he wasn't affected by the new restrictions on lighting up, but it bothered him that people's freedoms were eroding. Soon, there would be laws against wearing perfume and cooking in apartment buildings.

So yeah, smoking was stinky, and he preferred a smoke free environment, but it was a slippery slope, and he'd been to places around the world where this type of government over-reach went beyond absurd levels.

Like a death penalty for spitting on a sidewalk.

As he waited, the dance floor started filling up, and when

the first chord finally sounded, Gregg had to stretch his neck to see Alicia over the crowd.

Still, even from this distance, he could see her clearly, and his heart did a funny thing. It felt as if it flipped.

Rubbing his chest, he wondered whether everything was alright with his ticker. Was he experiencing heart palpitations or arrhythmia?

It wasn't an unfounded concern. He knew several guys around his age who had died from heart failure, and all of them had been programmers. Was there a connection?

He should get it checked.

"Welcome, everyone, and thank you for coming," Alicia said, then proceeded to introduce her band members, which he was happy to note were two more girls and one average-looking guy.

When the applause died out, Alicia started singing, and Gregg got lost in her voice. Raspy, sexy, and utterly unique, with an incredible vocal range.

What was she doing performing in a shitty nightclub like this? She should be a star.

The audience agreed with him, thanking the band with a deafening round of applause and then screaming for an encore at the end of the performance.

When several people climbed on the stage to buy CD's and ask for autographs, Gregg realized it was a good opportunity to approach Alicia.

"May I have your autograph?" He offered the back of his hand.

"Gregg. What are you doing here?"

"Listening to you sing. You're amazing."

"Thank you. Did Marcy tell you where I was performing?"

"I found you on Instagram. You were posting about this for the past two weeks."

She grinned. "Awesome. I'm so glad that you came."

"Me too. Do you need to leave right away? Or can I buy you a drink? It's nice out on the patio."

She glanced back at her band members. "Can you manage without me?"

"Go." The lead guitarist waved her on. "I'll take your stuff home."

"Thanks, Becca." Alicia sent her friend an air kiss.

"Do you and Becca live together?" Gregg asked.

"Yeah, and Raven too."

"What about Peter?"

She shook her head. "Not anymore. Peter and Raven used to be an item, but when they broke up, Peter moved out. It was just too awkward to have him sleeping on the living room couch."

"I bet." He took her hand and pulled her behind him to catch a table. "Quickly, before someone else snatches it."

Trotting behind him on her monster boots, Alicia laughed and started singing, "In the jungle, the mighty jungle, the lion needs a table tonight…"

They ordered drinks, and when they arrived, Gregg pulled the envelope out of his pocket and put it on the table.

"What's that?" Alicia asked.

"A gift certificate to a very special service."

His plan had been to ask her a million questions first and find out all he could about her fantasies, but for some reason, he'd opened up with the envelope.

Arching a brow, she pulled out the cream-colored card and looked at the title embossed in its center. Flipping it to the other side, she looked at the web address and the access code and then flipped it back to look at the front again.

"Are you hinting at something, Gregg? Because I don't get it."

"Don't tell me that you haven't heard of Perfect Match."

"Oh, I have. Everyone is talking about it. But why are you

giving me this? I heard it's super expensive, and it's not my birthday. Not that I would have accepted a gift like that from you no matter what the occasion. We don't even know each other well enough for such a personal and expensive gift."

"Would it make you feel better knowing that I didn't pay for it?"

"Maybe. How did you get it then?"

He hated mentioning that he owned a cybersecurity company, most often saying that he worked for one, but he just couldn't lie to Alicia when she was looking him straight in the eyes like this. He had a feeling she would know if he lied, or even if he fudged the truth a little.

"My partner and I did the encrypting for the Perfect Match servers when they were just starting out. They couldn't pay us what we asked for, so we agreed to take a big chunk of the compensation in gift certificates." He lifted the blue envelope. "We thought of it as being paid in stock or bonds. If the company succeeded, and we believed that it would, then these would appreciate in value, and they did."

"Why don't you sell them? If the gift certificates were part of the compensation for your services, then they weren't free."

"They were worth much less back then."

Alicia put her drink down and sighed. "Just tell me what this is all about, will you?"

He leaned toward her and took her hand. "Have you ever fantasized about the perfect adventure with the perfect lover?"

She chuckled. "Of course, I have. I'm a songwriter. I have a very creative imagination."

"Wouldn't you like to enact it?"

"With you?"

"With me, or with someone else. The algorithm will pair you with your perfect match. I just hope it will be me."

# 6

## ALICIA

*A*licia swallowed.

When Gregg had climbed up on the stage and asked for her autograph, she'd hoped he was finally going to ask her out, or at least flirt with her more directly. Maybe even try to seduce her into hooking up with him for the night.

Not that she would have done it.

Getting in bed with strangers was not her thing. Before getting naked with a guy, Alicia wanted to get to know him first, date him for a while, and fall in love with him at least a little bit.

That was why her list of lovers was so short. One serious boyfriend in college, and two later on. It had been more than a year since she'd had sex with anyone other than her battery-operated boyfriend, and frankly, she was quite fond of Bob. He didn't have mood swings that she had to tiptoe around, didn't make any demands on her time, was always ready for action, and didn't snore.

It didn't get much better than that, at least in her experience, but then it might in a virtual reality hookup.

PERFECT MATCH: CAPTAIN'S CONQUEST

It was like turning Bob into a real guy but still retaining all of his benefits.

"You're smiling." Gregg squeezed her hand.

She'd forgotten he was still holding it.

"That's good. Want to tell me what the smile is about?"

"Not really. What I want to know is what prompted this. You've been flirting with me for months, but you've never asked me out. Are you married?"

Hooking up via Perfect Match was the perfect way to cheat on a spouse without feeling overly guilty about it. After all, if she could reason herself into going for it by comparing the experience to having fun with her battery-operated boyfriend, then others could too. No one thought of using a sex toy as cheating.

"I'm not married, and I don't have a girlfriend. But I have to admit that I'm hooked on virtual hookups. I get to live out outrageous adventures risk-free, and with interesting partners that I would have never met otherwise. And once the fantasy is over, I can look forward to the next one without feeling guilty about disappointing anyone. It's exhilarating, liberating, and frankly, nothing in real life compares."

Aha. Now she understood. Gregg was a commitment-phob, and he was probably also emotionally stunted.

"Are you an engineer?"

She'd read somewhere that engineers typically scored higher than average on the autistic scale, which explained why many had trouble connecting with others outside of work.

"I have a masters in computer engineering. Why do you ask?"

Not wanting to offend him, she chose her words carefully. "Since you own a cybersecurity company, I figured that you must be a programmer, but typically engineers are not known for their vivid imaginations. How do you come up with the scenarios you want to enact in your Perfect Match adventures?"

He grinned. "Easy. I base them on movies and television shows. I'm a huge Star Trek fan, so many of my fantasies are about space exploration and landing on planets with fascinating cultures. The possibilities are endless."

For a long moment, she just stared at him. "What a coincidence. I'm a huge Star Trek fan too."

Gregg must have talked to Marcy or her other coworkers, and they had told him about her obsession.

"Which one? Original or Next Generation?" he asked.

"Next Generation."

"Picard or Kirk?"

"That depends. I liked Picard's command style, but he wasn't as sexy as Kirk, and he wasn't a ladies' man. But then the original show starring Kirk was done in a different era. Next Generation was more politically correct."

"They didn't eliminate the womanizer character completely, though. That's what they had Riker for. They split up Kirk's role, giving Picard the command and Riker all the fun stuff."

"True, but I wasn't a fan of Riker's."

"Who was your favorite?"

"Oh, it's hard to pick. I loved Data's childlike inquisitiveness and wonder. I liked Geordi's down-to-earth attitude, and I loved Deanna Troi's pretty much everything, including the hair. I liked Worf, and everyone else. In the old one, I loved Spock and Scotty the best."

"I meant as a love interest. Who did you fancy?"

She smirked. "Chris Pine playing as Captain Kirk in Star Trek Beyond."

Gregg grimaced. "It's those blue eyes. You know that he's wearing colored contact lenses, right?"

She huffed. "He is not. He's near-sighted and wears corrective contact lenses, not cosmetic ones."

# 7

# GREGG

*G*regg had gotten lucky. He would have never guessed that Alicia was a Star Trek fan.

Cool rocker chicks with tattoos and piercings didn't watch sci-fi shows. Only geeks like him did. But maybe Alicia was a geek in disguise?

Which meant that they had more in common than he'd suspected.

Except, it seemed that her ideal guy was blue-eyed and blond, while Gregg had dark brown eyes and dark brown hair. He was about the same height as the actor and had a similar athletic build, but that was where the similarities ended.

"What other actors do you find sexy?"

"Benedict Cumberbatch."

Damn. Another one with blue eyes, but at least he wasn't a blond.

"Who else?"

She smiled. "Why?"

He pointed at his face. "Brown eyes and brown hair here. I have to know if I'm your type."

"Except for your horrendous taste in clothes, you are every woman's type. Have you looked in the mirror lately?"

Now, that put a smile on his face. "You think I'm handsome?"

"Yes, but don't let it get to your head. I'm more interested in what's on the inside than what's on the outside."

"That's the right thing to say, but it's a big fat lie. Would you date an ugly guy even if he was the sweetest one on the planet?"

Her smile was sly. "I didn't say I was interested in sweet. And yes, I would have dated a smart ugly man if he had inner charisma and carried himself with confidence."

He crossed his arms over his chest. "Give me an example."

"Well, Cumberbatch is not exactly pretty, and I find Seal extremely appealing despite his scarred face, but then he has the silkiest voice."

"They are both handsome dudes."

"Yes, but not pretty."

"So other than sweet, which you said you weren't interested in, what other inner traits do you find desirable?"

"Brains, heart, honor, and guts."

"No cowards, then."

"Nope."

"And no liars."

"You got it."

It seemed that he had enough information to work with. What he didn't know, however, was what kind of adventure she envisioned, and what type of lover she preferred. But asking more questions would make his intent transparent.

Which wasn't a bad thing.

Then again, knowing everything took away from the sense of adventure. Maybe it was better to leave some things to chance.

"What about you?" Alicia asked. "Would you date an ugly woman if she was wonderful in every other way?"

"It depends on your definition of ugly. I would have no problem with odd looks or a scar or two, but that's about it. I like my ladies to be beautiful, but I'm not sold on a particular type."

"I want names. Actresses that you find sexy."

He laughed. "I'm weird. I adore Anne Hathaway because she has an awesome smile and a great voice. And I find Cate Blanchett sexy as hell even though she is too old for me."

It seemed that she liked his answers. "You are into unconventional beauties."

"I guess I am."

She tilted her head. "Do you find me attractive?"

"Insanely so. It hasn't been the coffee that had me coming to your Starbucks every day, and sometimes twice."

"Why didn't you just ask me out on a date? Why this?" She lifted the gift card.

"I don't date."

"Why is that?"

"Because I hate dating, and I'm not looking for a relationship." He pointed at the card. "From a purely pragmatic perspective, this is a much better way to find a partner. You can keep on searching until you find your perfect match, and no one gets their feelings hurt in the process."

"But you are not looking for a partner. You are in it for the virtual hookups."

"True, but if I happen to find my perfect match, I'll keep her."

"Is that why you are inviting me to do it? You want to see if we get matched up?"

"I hope we will."

For a long moment, Alicia just looked at him, but then she nodded. "Fine. I'll do it. How do we arrange it so we are paired?"

"We don't. You fill out a questionnaire on your end, and I

fill out one on mine. If we both choose a Star Trek adventure, the algorithm is more likely to match us."

"So, we won't know whether we were matched with each other or someone else, right? Not even after the adventure is over."

"If we choose avatars that look a lot different than us, then we won't know. But since we know each other, we can ask."

She shook her head. "If I do this, I don't want to know if it was you or not. I'll choose an avatar that doesn't look like me, and I won't answer your questions if you ask me about the experience."

"I can live with that."

Except, he wasn't going to change a damn thing about his appearance, so Alicia would know for sure that he was her partner and not some random dude.

Well, except maybe for the color of his eyes. He might ask for her favorite shade of blue.

8

# ALICIA

"*W*here is your not-so-secret admirer?" Marcy asked.

Alicia shrugged. "How should I know?"

"I thought that after he'd showed up at the club, things would move forward with you two."

The day after the concert, Alicia had told Marcy about Gregg and the drink they'd shared, but not about the Perfect Match gift certificate. It was too intimate. Some girlfriends shared details from the bedroom, but Alicia had never felt comfortable discussing her private life with others.

"Not really. We just talked."

"Yeah, and you found out that you were both Star Trek fans. I've seen relationships start with less than that."

Alicia grimaced. "Gregg made it very clear that he's not interested in a relationship, and I don't do hookups." Well, except for maybe virtual ones. She was still on the fence with that. "But even if he were interested in more than sex, I don't have time for something serious."

"Right." Marcy shook her head and then waved her hand. "Good riddance. He wasn't worth your time anyway."

It was nice of Marcy to say, and perhaps it was even true, but then Alicia was not rid of Gregg yet.

He might still be her perfect match. Not that she would know unless he made his avatar look like him, which was possible. The guy was gorgeous, why would he want to change his looks?

If asked, she wouldn't have changed anything about him. In fact, she'd been asked, and the perfect guy she'd described turned out a lot like Gregg.

Between the Star Trek fantasy that she'd concocted and the description of her perfect partner, the algorithm would pair them for sure.

Was that a good thing, though?

She'd realized that accepting the gift certificate had been a mistake the very next day when Gregg walked in and ordered his usual. Instead of the flirtatious banter they'd been enjoying for months, things had felt awkward.

Perhaps it had been only on her side, and she'd imagined the expectant gleam in Gregg's eyes and the stifled smirk on his lips, but the result was the same.

He'd stopped coming.

Perhaps instead of logging into Perfect Match's website the same night, she should have waited a day or two and considered the implications, but she'd been too excited and curious to wait.

First, she'd read the long explanation that attempted to explain in laymen's terms how the service worked, then she'd read the complete privacy guarantee, twice, and finally, she'd read about a hundred customer testimonials, raving about the experience.

It was two o'clock in the morning when she finished with that part and used the access code on her gift certificate to log in, register, and open the questionnaire.

If she had seen it first, she might have not used the access code. The questionnaire was very detailed and very intrusive, to the point that she'd felt herself blushing when answering some of the questions.

And yet, she'd kept at it even though her eyes had burned from lack of sleep.

It had been like a journey of self-discovery. She'd never pondered many of those questions, some of which had never even crossed her mind, and when forced to do so in order to provide honest answers, she'd been surprised by her own choices and preferences.

Had she been lying to herself her entire life?

Not really, she just hadn't been attuned to her inner self. It was disconcerting to realize that she tended to gloss over things that made her uncomfortable or things she disliked.

Alicia had filled up the questionnaire a week ago, but she'd never pressed the submit button.

Perhaps Gregg had already played out his Star Trek fantasy with someone else? There were plenty of fans out there.

Was that why he'd stopped showing up? Because he'd already found his perfect match?

On the one hand, it made her sad to think that Gregg was lost to her, but on the other hand, it made pressing that submit button much easier.

Perhaps her perfect match was somewhere out there, waiting for her to submit her questionnaire?

The thing was, thinking about that damn button had been stressing her out all week long, which was reason enough to just take the plunge and do it. Anyway, she wasn't going to use her own name or create an avatar that looked anything like her.

The name she'd chosen was Leia, not the Star War's princess, but a princess nonetheless. It was her fantasy after all, and if she wanted to be a princess voyaging through the stars with her favorite captain, she could.

# 9

# GREGG

"*I* knew it!" Gregg banged his fist on his desk.

More than a week had passed since Alicia had registered, but she hadn't submitted her questionnaire, and he was starting to think that she'd changed her mind.

Not wanting to push her, Gregg had stayed away from the Starbucks, waiting impatiently, anxious that the algorithm would pair him with someone else.

But as soon as she finally submitted it, the email informing him that a match had been found arrived less than an hour later.

He couldn't be a hundred percent sure it was her, and yet he was. Other than hacking into the system and manipulating the outcome, which would have been morally and legally wrong, he'd done everything else to ensure it. But the only information he'd allowed himself to hack into was whether she had completed her registration or not.

Right after he'd given Alicia the gift certificate, Gregg had gone home and filled out his questionnaire, making sure to submit it before she submitted hers. Star-Trek-themed fantasies were common for guys, and if not for his custom-tailored answers and descriptions, she might have been paired with someone else.

Since women favored different kinds of fantasies, the risk of the same happening to him was much lower.

According to Gabriel, and that was the only inside information he'd been willing to share, a guy had a much better chance of getting paired if he were ready to play a billionaire, a prince, a vampire, or a pirate.

Women were strange creatures, multifaceted, and with contradictory wishes and desires. Guys were so much simpler.

"Why do you look so smug?" Sam walked into his office. "Any good news?"

"Potentially."

"Care to share?"

"It's personal."

"Aha. You've booked another virtual hookup." Sam shook his head. "You have an addictive personality, my friend."

"Why would you say that? You've known me for years. I've gotten drunk precisely once, and I smoked one-third of a joint before deciding that I'm not going to touch the stuff ever again."

Pulling out a chair, Sam sat across from him. "I admit that none of your addictions are harmful, unless too much coffee and virtual sex are detrimental to your health."

"They are not." Gregg leaned back in his chair and crossed his arms over his chest. "You, on the other hand, are addicted to work. If not for Lisa, you would still be working eighteen-hour days. At least I know how to balance work with my hobbies."

Sam arched a brow. "What hobbies? The mountain climbing you do in an air-conditioned gym?"

Gregg huffed. "If you didn't keep bringing in more and more business, I could take more time off and go climbing real mountains."

"I doubt that. You are doing it to keep in shape because you hate weight training. What other hobbies do you have that I'm not aware of?"

"Sex, of course. Virtual and non-virtual."

Sam smirked. "As I said. You have a problem, buddy."

"I don't. I just haven't found the one woman to complete me yet." He put his hand over his chest and batted his eyelashes. "And until I do, I must keep searching."

# 10

# ALICIA

"*R*eady for your adventure?" the technician asked after attaching a gazillion wires to Alicia's body.

The top of her chest and her arms were covered with little squares of sticky pads, and she had a huge helmet thing hovering over her head. If this were a horror movie, this is what the victim of a mad scientist would look like.

Except, she was the mad one for doing this voluntarily.

"Let's go over the safety measures again," said the technician, whose name was Rebecca like Alicia's roommate but looked nothing like her.

By now, Alicia could recite them from memory, but she nodded politely and answered questions until the tech was satisfied that they had covered everything safety related.

"Anything you want to ask me before we proceed?" Rebecca asked.

"Are you sure that, once I enter the virtual world, I'm not going to remember who I am? How can that be? Where do all my memories go?"

The tech patted her knee. "Your memories are still there.

They are not going anywhere. Think of it as a movie that is superimposed over your brain. Once the movie ends and the feed stops, you'll have access to all of your old memories and also the new ones from your awesome adventure."

"Has anyone woke up not remembering his or her life from before?"

"No, but I've had quite a few customers who were very unhappy about returning to reality. They wanted to stay in dreamland forever."

According to the manual, the entire session was going to be three hours long, but supposedly time moved differently in the virtual world, which meant that during those three hours, it could feel as if weeks or even months had passed.

Provided it was fun, it could be great to enjoy a vacation from her mundane life. But what if it was not fun? What if she ended up hating her adventure?

"Has anyone had a bad experience?"

Rebeca shook her head. "The way the program is designed, it can't happen. If the sensors detect distress, the algorithm will adjust the story. Everyone gets their happy ending no matter how outrageous the adventure leading up to it is."

That was reassuring.

Taking a deep breath, Alicia nodded. "I'm ready."

"What's your avatar's name?"

"Princess Leia." Alicia smiled sheepishly, wondering how many women before her had chosen that name and title.

"Very well." Rebecca didn't react to it one way or another.

She put a set of goggles over Alicia's eyes and lowered the helmet, adjusting it so it fit snugly. "I'm going to count back from ten. Ten, nine, eight…"

# 11

# ALICIA

## AKA PRINCESS LEIA

"*I*'m deeply honored to be chosen for this mission." Leia bowed to her mother.

The queen hid a smile by dipping her head. "It is a great day for our people." She pushed to her feet and motioned for Leia to follow. "Come, daughter. I have a few last words to impart before your departure, and I wish to do so in private."

"Of course."

Good. The stifling formality was necessary for the sake of the news reporters who had been treating this like a freaking reality show. Ever since news of the Krall's ancestral home planet discovery had spread, their court had been overrun with news crews from all over the world.

Until Leia actually stepped onto the transporter platform and got beamed up with the rest of the delegation, she had to contend with them following her everywhere.

Thankfully, the interstellar ship's captain had refused them entry.

"We don't have much time," her mother sat on the couch and patted the spot next to her.

"We've been over everything a thousand times, mom. I'm well prepared, and so are the rest of the delegates."

"I know, but I can't help worrying. We are very different people now than we were five hundred years ago when our ancestors woke up from their millennia-long frozen sleep under the ice. Those on the home planet still have the same superior attitude toward other races, and they might look down on you and the other delegates because you are more human than Krall. Even worse, they might lust after your blood."

Leia reached for her mother's hand. "I've majored in Krall history. I know what I'm up against."

Her mother smiled. "History books put a positive spin on things. You might discover that our people are more elitist and their customs more barbaric than what's in those books."

Snorting, Leia let go of her mother's hand and crossed her arms over her chest. "We still keep some of those so-called barbaric customs."

Not everyone practiced the old mating rituals, but as the queen's daughter, Leia was expected to follow the tradition.

"They are not nearly as barbaric as they used to be," her mother said. "Before taking human consorts and absorbing human customs, Krall couples met only to procreate, and those were vicious encounters. The children were raised by their mothers alone, with the fathers expected to contribute financially to their upbringing but nothing else. Thankfully, the Krall mating rituals got softened by those of humans. What we have today is a meshing of both traditions."

"And genetics. We've lost the special mental powers of our ancestors, but at least we no longer have to drink blood for sustenance."

Raw meat was still considered a delicacy, but other than that the Krall ate the same artificially produced foods as the rest of Earth Federation's population.

Their arctic circle territory was no longer secluded and isolated from the rest of the world, but they retained their autonomy to some extent. While Earth was ruled by a group of elected officials from the different continents, the Krall held on to their monarchy, even though nowadays it was mostly ceremonial in nature.

There were no pure-blooded Krall left and, with the exception of a few individuals, the mental powers their ancestors had possessed were mostly extinct. The new Krall were also not as striking as their forefathers and foremothers had been, but since the Krall black hair and black eyes were determined by a dominant gene, their descendants retained the coloring even though they were genetically more human than Krall.

"I hope that won't be a problem on the home planet," her mother said. "You should make it very clear from the get-go that none of the delegates are to be used as snacks."

Leia laughed. "The Krall council is well aware of that. They've been informed that we no longer drink blood straight from the vein."

Her mother waved an impatient hand. "They might think that they can get away with hypnotizing you into compliance. Your human blood will sing to them."

"It's going to be okay. I'm immune to hypnotic influence, and the other delegates know to stay close to me."

This was the one time that Leia was glad her Krall genetics were less diluted than most, which made her resistant to mind manipulation. Regrettably, those genes also made her taller than most human females and provided her with fangs. Not the long canines of the vast majority of this generation of Krall, but actual fangs.

When she wanted to go places incognito, Leia had to remember to keep her mouth closed.

Her mother produced a chip from her pocket and handed it to Leia. "This long trip provides a perfect opportunity to ponder your choices of suitable mates. I had my secretary compile a dossier on each of the available noble sons. When you come back, you really can't delay issuing a summons."

Barely managing to stifle a grimace, Leia nodded politely. "That's very thoughtful of you. Thank you."

She had no intention of choosing one of the Krall nobles as her mate, and she didn't need her mother's secretary to compile a dossier for her. There weren't many of them, and Leia knew each one personally. She'd rather stay an old maiden than summon one of them.

Her mother patted her knee. "If we weren't so far removed genetically from our ancestors, perhaps you could've found a suitable mate on the home planet."

Leia snorted. "You've just warned me that they might be interested in me as a snack."

"I was speaking hypothetically." The queen smiled. "Out of all the noble sons, which ones are you considering for the summons?"

"None."

The smile melted off her mother's face. "You have to choose, Leia. How about Meroll?"

Did she have to pick the worst one? "Anyone but him."

It was bad enough that he'd been chosen as one of the delegates. She'd tried to argue against it, but Meroll's house was powerful, and other than personal dislike she couldn't come up with a good excuse to have him disqualified.

"Why? I remember you being quite infatuated with him."

"That was ten years ago, and my so-called infatuation lasted for about two weeks. I was sixteen, and Meroll looked good in an Interstellar Fleet uniform, but even then, I knew he wasn't a good person. Maybe that's why he never made captain even though he finished top of his class."

The queen grimaced. "There is still a lot of prejudice against us. That's why Meroll was never promoted, and that was why he eventually quit the fleet."

Leia doubted that had been the reason. Meroll was an arrogant asshole, and no one liked him. Not the type of personality suitable for an Interstellar ship's captain.

Jacques Kirk, now that was another story.

He'd finished second in class, not first, but Leia had known even back then that he was going to surpass Meroll and achieve greatness.

It hadn't been intuition or some other mystical foreknowledge that had brought about this conviction. Even at sixteen, Leia could recognize that special quality that made someone a leader, and Kirk had it. He'd been everyone's favorite, and that included her.

After the graduation ceremony, her infatuation had switched from Meroll to Jacques, but unlike the first one, the second hadn't waned over time.

Ten years later, her heart still made a little flip every time his name was mentioned.

"What if I summon a human mate?" Leia blurted.

"I guess it would be okay if you choose a man from our territory. There are still some pure humans left. But I'm afraid that those from other parts of the world would not understand our ways."

"What if he did? Would you be okay with that?"

"I would prefer for you to preserve our bloodline and mate a Krall, but I can't prohibit you from summoning a human. We can't afford to appear discriminatory."

"I think it would be good for our reputation, and that's more important than bloodline. Perhaps if I mate an outsider, maybe someone well-known, it would lessen the prejudice against us."

"Do you have anyone in mind?"

"Not really. I was just mulling over the idea."

It was a lie. Leia did have a particular human in mind, but until recently, Jacques hadn't known that she existed. Now that she was about to board his ship, he probably had read up on the little-known Princess Leia of the Krall. But he still didn't know Leia the person. Not yet, anyway.

She intended to change that.

"Fortunately, this voyage gives us time to ponder the possibilities." The queen pushed up from the couch and pulled Leia into her arms. "I'm going to miss you."

"I'm coming back in four months. I've been gone longer than that before."

While getting her masters in inter-planetary relations, Leia had only returned home twice.

"Yes, that's true. But the Mars colony is close to home. I knew I could hop on a transport and come to visit you anytime I wanted. Now you are going to travel light years away."

# 12

# GREGG

## AKA CAPTAIN JACQUES KIRK

"The Krall delegation is ready for transport, Captain."
Jack's new security officer stood at attention, her
back straight, her shoulders back, and her eyes focused somewhere over his left shoulder.

After all the years B'Kala had spent in the academy,
mingling with humans and a dozen or so other species, she was
still a Kongelian through and through. Which was a good
thing. She was fierce and strong, and there wasn't much she
couldn't handle.

Except for a friendly smile or some indication that she
found his jokes funny.

But then nobody was perfect.

"Lead the way, Commander B'Kala."

"Yes, sir."

Jack stopped next to the ship's counselor. "Commander
Vugg, you are with us."

Dealing with the Krall delegates was going to be a pain in
the ass, but Vugg's calming influence was going to help.

The one Krall Jack had the displeasure of knowing had been
a fellow cadet at the Interstellar Academy, and the guy had

39

been a conceited, self-absorbed bastard. The fact that Meroll had gotten the best grades, or that all the female cadets had drooled over him, hadn't helped endear him to the other male cadets, and especially not to Jack.

After Meroll had quit Interstellar Fleet, Jack had hoped never to see the bastard again, but fate had other ideas. Jack's ship had been the only one scheduled to arrive home in time to pick up the delegation, and the voyage to the Krall planet wasn't a big detour from where he needed to be next.

Meroll's name appearing on the list of delegates hadn't even been a big surprise. Not only did the guy come from one of the leading Krall noble houses, but he was also uniquely suited to play the role of a smooth-talking politician.

Hopefully, the other Krall delegates weren't as bad, but given their reputation, there was little chance of that. They were no longer called the demon horde, and the current generation was genetically mostly human, but people had long memories, and the sins of their ancestors were never going to be forgotten.

"Put a smile on your face," Vugg said quietly. "You look like you have a sour taste in your mouth."

"I have no experience dealing with royalty. And if Princess Leia is anything like Meroll, then she is going to be a royal pain in the ass."

On his other side, B'Kala retained her impassive expression, but he'd caught the slight twitching of the corner of her lips.

So, the Kongelian had a sense of humor after all.

"You've seen the news. She is soft-spoken, eloquent, and a knockout." Vugg smiled. "If the princess gets on your nerves, I'll gladly take her off your hands. Alternatively, you can endure by imagining her naked."

He had done that already. But he wasn't going to admit it. A typical Krall, the princess was tall, with dark olive skin and black glossy hair. What he found most appealing, though, were her tiny fangs.

In the interview he'd watched, Leia had done her damnedest not to let them show as she talked, but he'd caught a peek, and for some inexplicable reason, the sight had gotten him hard.

And that was another reason to dread the hosting of the damn delegation. Lusting after the Krall princess was unacceptable.

"Captain." Thomas saluted as they entered the transporter room. "The delegation's luggage was delivered to their quarters."

"Thank you, Lieutenant."

Marina, the other crew member he'd assigned to see to the delegates' needs, looked bothered.

"Is there a problem, Ensign?"

"I added the raw meat program to the dispenser, but it looks and tastes off."

"Don't worry about it. They can eat regular food."

"Yes, sir."

Jack turned to the transporter's operator. "Whenever you are ready, Lieutenant Bronson."

"We are ready to initiate transport," the lieutenant announced.

"Five to beam up," his counterpart on Earth replied.

"Initiate." Bronson tapped the display.

Jack watched as the five figures materialized, ignoring Meroll and focusing on the one in the center.

The princess, in her full royal regalia, looked formidable and stunningly beautiful. In person, she was much more impressive than on screen or even on the holo-projector.

"Welcome to the Orion, Princess Leia." He walked over to the platform and waited for her to step down. "Captain Jacques Kirk." He offered her his hand.

The smile that spread over the princess's face softened her features, making her appear more approachable, more human. "Thank you for granting us passage on your ship, Captain. In the name of the Krall, I thank you." She bowed her head in the manner of her people.

For her, he would keep up the pretense of having been given a choice and magnanimously agreeing. "Welcome aboard. It is my duty and my pleasure."

Leia nodded. "Let me introduce my fellow delegates."

"You know Meroll of house Progall. You two graduated from the academy together."

"Good to see you, Kirk." Meroll offered his hand, the haughty grimace on his face belying his friendly greeting.

"Same here." Jack shook the hand he'd been offered. "So, what have you been up to since leaving the fleet?"

Meroll smirked. "I find politics much more intriguing."

# 13

# LEIA

*a*s Leia caught herself staring into Jack's blue mesmerizing eyes, she forced her head to turn and looked at her fellow delegate whose hand Jack was now shaking.

Humans had such variety of color, while the Krall, even after many generations of intermarriage, all shared the same boring dark colors. Maybe that was the reason their traditional robes were so brightly colored. It provided the variety and individuality that nature did not.

But even among humans, Jack's eyes were unique. She hadn't seen any of such vivid turquoise color, and his hair wasn't just some old plain brown either. It was a warm chestnut. He was very tall for a human, and the formal dress uniform complimented his athletic build, showcasing his broad shoulders.

A truly fine male in every respect.

Would her mother approve of her issuing him an invitation?

Now that she was standing in front of him, though, her plan to do so seemed silly. It had been a girl's wishful thinking, and not the calculated decision of a grown woman who was also a political figure.

Unlike her friends, Leia wasn't free to choose a mate.

Most humans were not familiar with Krall nobility's mating ritual. At best, the Captain would find it odd; at worst, he would regard it as barbaric.

His security officer, on the other hand, would understand. The Kongelian practiced similar rituals.

Once the delegates had all shaken hands with the captain, Jack turned to Leia. "Let me introduce my security officer. Commander B'Kala of the house of Torgas."

Leia had heard the name during her studies. The commander's house was an old and respected one.

"I'm honored to meet a daughter of the house of Torgas," Leia said as they shook hands. "Your line is legendary."

The commander smiled, her sharp teeth gleaming white. "The honor is all mine, Princess Leia of the Krall."

From her studies on the Kongelians, Leia knew that they smiled only on two occasions; when greeting someone they were hoping to befriend, or when issuing a challenge. She was quite sure that the commander intended the first and not the second, but perhaps later on she could ask B'Kala to train with her.

Leia smiled back and tightened her hand on B'Kala's, letting her feel the strength of her grip. She was an accomplished fighter, but she'd never sparred with a Kongelian before.

It would be interesting to compare techniques.

Heck, who was she fooling? Leia wanted to see if she could beat the security officer in hand to hand combat.

Human females were no challenge for Leia, nor were most of the Krall whose blood was much more diluted than hers.

But a Kongelian, now that was a challenge,

"And this is Counselor Vugg," the captain said.

The counselor looked human, but his name suggested that he was of Akonian descent.

"Princess Leia, it is an honor to meet you." He offered her his hand.

"The honor is mine, commander."

Once all the introductions were finally done, Jack gestured with his hand toward the exit. "Let me escort you to your quarters, Princess Leia."

She followed him out of the transporter room and into a wide hallway, her fellow delegates and several crew members walking a few steps behind them.

"Thank you, Captain."

"Please call me Jack."

"Not Jacques?"

"I prefer Jack."

"Then you must call me Leia. Every time someone says princess, I look over my shoulder thinking they are referring to someone else."

"Really?" As he grinned, two dimples formed in his cheeks, making him look devilishly handsome. "You don't use the title at home?"

"Only in official ceremonies, and those are few and far between."

"I thought your people were big on formality."

"We used to be. Very few of the old customs are still observed, and only by the nobility."

He cast a quick glance behind his shoulder at Meroll. "In preparation for your arrival, I've read a little about your history. Not much is known."

"We are a secretive people."

"Yes, that was one of the things mentioned. Which, obviously, made me even more curious about you." He stopped in front of a double door. "Here we are. The keypad is ready for your voice input."

As she programmed the door to respond to her voice commands, her fellow delegates continued down the hallway to their assigned quarters.

Only Meroll glanced at her and the captain and then frowned.

"Would you like to come in?" Leia asked as the doors opened.

She could practically feel Meroll's eyes burning holes in her back.

Jack nodded and followed her inside. "I hope you find your accommodations satisfactory."

Taking a long look around, she chuckled. "What is this, the royal suite?" She hadn't expected such lavish quarters on a starship.

"Indeed, it is. As your title implies, you are a royal."

"My title is pretty meaningless. We are part of the Earth Federation. The monarchy is symbolic."

"Perhaps, but I think your distant relatives were very impressed that a princess was sent as the chief delegate."

"About that. The report we were given on them was far from complete. I was hoping you would know more and could debrief me on the way."

He nodded. "If it's agreeable to you, after you settle in, of course, I would like to invite you to dine in my quarters, and we can talk over dinner. I had the chef prepare a special meal for you and your fellow delegates."

That was disappointing. She'd hoped to spend some time alone with the captain.

"They would dine with my officers, of course."

*Much better.*

For a brief moment, Leia debated whether she should change out of her traditional robes. She'd donned them for the live televised broadcast of the delegation's departure. She looked good in them, the bright colors complimenting her natural ones, but they were cumbersome, regal, and designed to intimidate.

Except, if she ever decided to go ahead with her crazy plan, and summon Jack to a mating ritual, it was all about the female intimidating the hell out of her chosen male and fighting him every step of the way.

To have her, he would have to prove himself worthy.

"I don't need to settle in. If you are ready, we can dine right away."

Jack grinned, the two dimples making a reappearance. "I was hoping you'd say that. I'm ravenous."

# 14

## JACK

"*T*hen we should definitely not delay, Captain."

Given the slight smirk lifting one corner of Leia's lush, red-colored lips, she hadn't missed his double entendre.

Jack's raging attraction to the Krall princess was totally unexpected. Nevertheless, he should have refrained from making suggestive comments. It was inappropriate and could get him in a lot of trouble, but unless he was completely off, Leia was sending him signals that she was interested.

Nothing was overt, and he might have seen what he wanted to see, but the way she had looked at him, and the way her voice had gotten just a little huskier when she talked to him couldn't have been just his imagination.

When they got to his quarters, Leia paused at the entrance. "I hope you didn't give up your suite for me. This one is not half as lavish as the one I'm staying in."

He motioned for her to follow him to the dining table. "I'm a single man, and my needs are modest. The guest suite is designed to accommodate a family or a dignitary with several servants." He pulled out a chair for her.

"I see." Leia arranged her robes before sitting down.

He loved the way she moved, so graceful and elegant. Did finishing schools for princesses still exist?

"I let the chef know that we are ready to dine," he said as he sat across from her.

"I thought that everything aboard an interstellar ship came from dispensers."

"It does. But we have a chef who is in charge of programming it, and from time to time she likes to prepare meals for special occasions the traditional way."

"I would hate to trouble her. I have no problem with dispenser meals. The imitation never tastes exactly as the original, but it's close enough."

He waved a hand. "Moria would have been mad for being denied the pleasure of preparing a special welcome meal for the delegation."

Leia dipped her head. "In this case, I'm looking forward to sampling her cuisine."

"Can I offer you a drink while we wait for dinner to be served? We've programmed the dispenser with several Krall favorites."

She smiled. "I would like to try something new. Can you offer a suggestion?"

"What kind of drinks do you like?"

"I have a high tolerance for alcohol, so I would like something potent, but I also have a very discriminating taste, so I would like a sophisticated flavor that will take me by surprise."

Had the drink description been meant as a double entendre? Was the princess flirting with him? Or was he interpreting everything she said through the prism of his own attraction to her?

Jack chuckled. "Well, that rules out Kongelian brews. Potent as the fires of hell, but not exactly sophisticated."

As he pushed to his feet, Leia glanced around. "Can you

point me toward the facilities? I would like to freshen up before dinner."

"The second door on the left."

"Thank you."

As Leia ducked into the bathroom, Jack walked over to the dispenser and ordered their drinks. "Two Monrevian twisters on ice."

As they materialized, the doorbell chimed.

"Enter." He took the drinks to the table.

A young Ensign rolled in a cart. "May I set the table, Captain?"

"Thank you, Ensign, but that won't be necessary. You can leave the cart, and I'll take care of the rest." Having the guy hovering over them throughout dinner would have been annoying.

"Yes, Captain."

As the door closed behind the ensign, Jack removed the lids from the first course and put the plates on the table. Next went the napkins and the silverware.

"Did I miss Moria?" Leia asked.

"Moria doesn't serve the meals she prepares. I told the ensign to leave the cart."

Once again, Jack pulled out the chair for Leia. "I've read that male Krall regard it as an honor to feed their females."

Leia stifled a laugh. "It's part of the courtship ritual. Are you courting me, Jack?"

She was surprisingly blunt, and he picked up the gauntlet even though he shouldn't have. "Would you be averse to my courtship?"

He was out of line, but on the other hand, Leia wasn't part of his crew, and she wasn't a subordinate. There were no rules against them having a fling during her voyage.

Lifting her drink, she took a small sip and then put it down.

"Not at all. But I'm afraid that you don't know what's involved. Otherwise, you wouldn't have offered to court me so casually."

# 15

# LEIA

*T*hings were progressing much faster than Leia had ever hoped. She'd been flirting lightly, just to test the waters and see whether Jack showed an interest in her, but it seemed she was at an impasse.

Now, she either had to back out and make light of the direction their conversation had taken them, or come out and offer Jack a summons.

It was too soon for that, though. He didn't know her yet, didn't care for her, and he wasn't a Krall who would have been honor-bound to accept.

"Then tell me," Jack said. "You've whetted my curiosity, and now I have to know."

Smiling, she waved a dismissive hand. "It's too serious a subject to joke about."

He didn't smile back. "Who is joking? I'm dead serious."

"Why? You don't know me. Why would you want to court a woman you've just met?"

"Isn't it obvious? We are both single, you are a stunningly beautiful woman, smart, fascinating, and to say that I am attracted to you is putting it mildly. What else is there?"

She sighed. "I am not free to indulge in casual relations, Jack. When the time comes for me to summon a male, it will be for the purpose of finding a worthy mate. A husband is a term you are more familiar with."

His eyes widened. "Does summoning a male mean what I think it does?"

"I don't know what you are thinking, so I can't answer your question."

He shook his head. "Pardon me, but it seems I have no choice but to ask this directly. Am I to understand that you have never invited a man into your bed?"

She nodded. "Correct."

"Why?"

"Because I am the princess, and I'm expected to uphold tradition, which is a mixture of Krall and human customs. My ancestors didn't have anything resembling marriage. When a female wished to have a child, she summoned a suitable male. He was honor obligated to accept and then prove himself worthy of fathering her child. They didn't stay together. If the union was fruitful, and a child was born, the father was expected to contribute financially, but the female raised the child alone."

"So, sex was only for procreation?"

"Between the Krall, yes, but because the fertility rate was low, many summonses had to be issued before pregnancy was achieved."

"I see. So, it was okay to indulge in the name of conception. Did the females keep summoning the same male until they conceived, or did they switch between partners?"

"It was one male per fertile season, which was more or less two weeks out of every three months. Establishing paternity was important."

"Obviously."

"When the Krall started taking on human consorts, they

were introduced to human mating customs, and the two got meshed together. The initial summoning by the female was still done the same way, but if the male proved worthy, the couple got married and stayed together to raise their children. In time, the summoning was mostly abandoned as well. Only the noble houses still observe that tradition."

"Are you expected to remain chaste until you summon a mate?"

"Chastity is the result, not the impetus. I can't be with a man without issuing a summons, but I can only issue a summons for the purpose of choosing a permanent mate."

# 16

# JACK

"Interesting custom." Jack rubbed his jaw.

Archaic, that was for sure. Virginity was something most young people wanted to be rid of as soon as possible. A woman Leia's age should have been with a long line of lovers by now.

Jack found himself torn between two contradicting emotions. On the one hand, he pitied Leia for being a slave to outdated customs. But on the other hand, he experienced a most surprising caveman-like excitement at the prospect of being her first.

Except, that meant marriage, and it wasn't what Jack had in mind when he'd started flirting with the princess, or rather responding to her subtle cues.

Was she interested in him as a potential husband?

Now that was a shocker.

He was a confident guy, but he wasn't prince material. Perhaps she was one of those women who had a thing for uniforms?

A captain's post on an Interstellar ship was no small

achievement either. Maybe that was what she was impressed by?

Shifting in her chair, Leia picked up her glass. "Yes, well. It is what it is, and there isn't much I can do about it." She sighed. "I am bound by tradition." She straightened her shoulders and smiled, slipping into her princess persona with practiced ease. "Let's talk about something else. What happened to the Krall? Did they explain why they had abandoned their people on Earth?"

Unsure how he felt about the princess's matrimonial interest, Jack was glad for the change of subject. "They didn't abandon you. The truth is that they had no idea you existed."

"How is it possible?"

"No one knows for sure, but we have a hypothesis. Those on Earth were most likely sent to colonize the planet, but the ice age ended their food supply, and they were forced into frozen sleep. In the meantime, their home planet must have suffered a major catastrophe. Perhaps it was a massive solar storm that destroyed their infrastructure, wiping out all of their technology and all of their knowledge base that must have been stored electronically, much in the same way ours was several hundred years ago. But unlike us, the Krall were isolated, and their accumulated knowledge hadn't been stored off planet like ours is. Most of their population must have died of famine, and they were basically thrown back to the Stone Age. It has taken them thousands of years to rebuild, and they are not there yet. Their current technology is at the level Earth's was before the discovery of space folding, which means that their space travel is limited to their solar system."

Leia shook her head. "Perhaps it wasn't a natural disaster."

"The other hypothesis is that the planet we discovered is not their original home but another colony. And just as you lost the knowledge of your origins, so did they. Except, their planet had no other intelligent humanoid species like Earth."

"Do they have mythology? Maybe a religion that hints at what happened?"

He smiled. "That's one of the reasons you are heading there. To find out. They weren't very forthcoming during initial contact."

She nodded. "The secretive nature must be hardwired into our genes. If they had to restart from nothing, their new culture could've developed in a completely different direction than the old one my ancestors brought with them to Earth. I guess my study of Krall history is not going to be all that helpful."

"As an Interstellar fleet captain, I have some experience in dealing with newly discovered civilizations. I'll gladly assist in any capacity you may deem useful."

"Thank you."

# 17

# LEIA

*A*s they ate in silence, Leia was grateful for the many years she'd spent in her mother's court, practicing an impassive expression and hiding her feelings.

Her girly fantasies had been shattered.

Obviously, Jack's interest in her was limited to a casual voyage fling. He wasn't impressed with her enough to consider marriage, and that was even before he knew what was involved in courting a Krall princess.

What a colossal disappointment, especially since she wanted him now more than ever.

The more time she spent with Jack, the more convinced she became that he was the one for her. Captain Jacques Kirk had everything she desired in a mate.

His charismatic personality was matched by keen intelligence and a powerful body, and yet he wasn't condescending or full of himself. Jack's friendly and respectful attitude toward his crew impressed her. That was how Leia interacted with her people and how she wanted her husband to interact with them as well.

That wasn't going to happen with Meroll or any of the other stuck-up noble sons.

Her mother had drilled into her head that her marriage was not going to be a romantic affair, and that she should focus on finding a mate who was a suitable future king. Her personal likes and dislikes were supposed to take a back seat to that.

Except, Jack fulfilled both criteria beautifully. There wasn't a single thing Leia didn't like about him, and he would make a fine mate and someday a fine king.

Her mother wasn't stepping down anytime soon, so it wasn't as if Jack would have to give up his career in the Interstellar fleet. If twenty years or so from now he had to choose between becoming the fleet's admiral or some other high-ranking position, or retiring and taking on royal duties, they could address it then.

Politically, it was a good move as well. Jack marrying her would do wonders for her people's reputation.

Besides, the thought of settling for one of the nobles' sons made Leia's skin crawl, especially if she was forced to mate Meroll. As the son of the most powerful house, he was expecting a summons from her.

Leia would rather abdicate her title, but unfortunately, she was an only child. In her absence, Meroll, who was a distant cousin and next in line, would become king without having to mate her.

Which meant that giving up was not an option. Jack had to be hers.

Lifting her eyes from the plate, Leia stared at him until he looked up as well. "I might take you up on your offer."

Jack put his fork down. "I'm at your service, Princess Leia. Anything you need, I am your man."

She stifled a smile. Jack had backed himself into a corner, and she wasn't going to miss this opportunity to pounce on him. "I hope that you are a man of your word, Captain Jacques Kirk."

He frowned. "Is there a reason you are questioning my honor?"

"Not yet. But what I'm about to ask you may cause you to go back on your word."

Smiling, he pretended to glance around. "I don't see any dragons you might want me to slay or Guntavian eagles to subdue."

She chuckled. "You are sitting across from one."

Affecting a mock frown, Jack shook his head. "I'm confused, and that doesn't happen often. As far as I know, the Krall are not shape-shifters."

"We are not, and I'm not a lady dragon or a Guntavian eagle, but I want you to wrestle me, and I'm one hell of a fighter."

For a moment, Jack just stared at her, then he cleared his throat and picked up a napkin to wipe his mouth although there was nothing to clean. "My apologies, Princess, but I do not wrestle with females, and it has nothing to do with misogyny. I wouldn't spar with B'Kala, even though we are probably equally matched in strength and skill. It's too intimate and might lead to impropriety."

# JACK

With a sly smile, Leia leaned back in her chair and crossed her arms over her chest. "That's what I'm counting on."

As thoughts of wrestling the nude princess in bed flitted through his mind, Jack became painfully hard. And the worst part was that he couldn't adjust himself without revealing his predicament.

What kind of game was she playing with him? And what was happening to her?

The woman sitting across from him wasn't the same one who had followed him into his quarters, the one he had spent a pleasant evening with, talking about politics and customs.

Up until this moment, Leia's flirting had been subtle, and she seemed so reasonable, so worldly and sophisticated. She'd shed that skin, revealing the predator lurking underneath.

It wasn't just about the tiny fangs peeking out of her mouth as she smiled suggestively. Her entire demeanor had changed, and she was practically crackling with sexual energy.

If he were a lesser man, he might have been put off by the

aggressive undertones, but Jack loved a challenge, and if he weren't mistaken, Leia had just thrown one at him.

Folding his napkin, he put it over his knee and leaned back, affecting the same nonchalant pose as Leia. "I'm a simple man, Princess. And I'm afraid that I'm not good at interpreting hints even if they hit me over the head. If you need my help with something, you will have to spell it out for me. What exactly is it that you want me to do?"

Her bravado faltering, Leia looked away and let out a breath. "This isn't easy for me."

Her admission made him feel like an ass. Leia wasn't a fellow cadet at the academy that he was competing with, and he should have been more gentle with her.

"Would another drink help?"

She nodded. "I'm not a big believer in liquid courage, but I could certainly use any help I can get for what I'm about to tell you."

His curiosity piqued, Jack walked over to the dispenser. "Same one as before?"

"Yes, please. I liked it."

When the drinks were ready, he carried them back to the table and sat down. "You'll find me a very good listener. I'm open-minded, and I'm not judgmental."

"That's good." She took the tall glass and waited for the fumes to disperse before taking a long sip. "As I've hinted before, I'm expected to summon a mate. In fact, I've been delaying doing so for the last four years, and the pressure is mounting."

"I can understand your reluctance to settle down. You are still a young woman. What's the rush?"

"Tradition. I'm supposed to produce an heir, and since I'm an only child, there is pressure to hurry up and do it. It's not that I'm averse to marriage or to motherhood." She chuckled sadly. "I'm not made from stone, and I crave intimacy, but my selection of suitable husbands leaves a lot to be desired. And if you think I'm finicky, let me point out that Meroll is at the top of that list. The sons of the other Krall noble houses are not much better, and in some respects even worse. At least Meroll is ambitious and accomplished. Some of the others are spoiled rich boys who have done nothing with their lives."

Poor princess. No wonder she didn't want to get married. Spinsterhood was preferable to being tied to the likes of Meroll, but he couldn't tell her that. Leia had an obligation to her people.

"Meroll is indeed very accomplished." Saying that felt like chomping on glass shards.

She arched a brow. "I know that you can't stand him, and I share the same sentiment."

"What gave you that impression?"

Jack had been just as cordial to Meroll as to the other delegates and wondered what had given him away.

"I was at your graduation ceremony, and I watched you two. You were not as good at hiding your feelings back then."

He frowned. "I don't remember seeing you there."

"I was sixteen, and I didn't do anything to attract attention to myself. I came with Meroll's family, and you probably thought I was his sister or cousin."

"I ignored the entire bunch. How come you came with them, though?"

Leia shook her head. "Unbelievably, I had a crush on Meroll, or rather on his uniform. But it didn't take me long to realize how obnoxious and condescending he was toward his fellow cadets, especially when compared to you." She smiled. "You were like a sun, illuminating everyone with your inner light and warmth, while he was like a black hole, sucking out everyone's positive energy."

"I'm flattered, but I think you are exaggerating a bit. I wasn't all sunshine and smiles, and Meroll wasn't all darkness and gloom. He had his good days."

Not really, but it was the right thing to say. Jack couldn't remember one instance of Meroll helping another cadet over a hurdle. That alone should have disqualified him, but he belonged to an influential family, and they would have screamed discrimination if he'd been kicked out. With Meroll's excellent grades and stellar performance, it would have been a tough case proving that he lacked the social skills necessary for a fleet officer. If his family sued, they might have won.

Leia picked up her drink and took a long sip before putting it down again. "The day of your graduation, my crush moved from Meroll to you, and it has stayed with you ever since."

Talk about a shocker. The princess had a ten-year-long crush on him?

"I don't know what to say."

"Don't say anything. I'm not done yet." She let out a breath. "And that was the easiest thing to admit. I'm not saying that I'm in love with you. I'm not sixteen anymore, and I know that a crush is not love. But I still think that you are the best man I've ever met, and I still want you as my mate. You are not obligated to respond to my summons as a Krall male would have been, and I know that in human culture it is more common for the male to propose, but I would like you to consider it."

Jack had been propositioned before, multiple times, but never with marriage.

He dipped his head. "I'm honored."

What else could he have said?

When he opened his mouth to voice his many buts, Leia lifted a hand to stop him. "Don't give me your answer yet. There is more."

Curious, he arched a brow. "Go on."

"There is more at stake than just my marital bliss or lack thereof. The Krall's reputation is of a stuck-up people who look down on the rest of humanity even though genetically we are now more human than Krall. And our ancestors enslaving yours and using them as involuntary blood donors has never been forgotten either. I believe that our mating would help change all that. The future queen mating a human, a well-known and respected Interstellar fleet captain, would be big news and a chance for us to put a positive spin on our culture."

The princess wasn't pulling punches. He was still trying to process her proposal on a personal level. Adding global implication wasn't making it any easier.

Lifting the glass, she emptied the drink down her throat, shook her head, and grimaced. "Wow, this is potent." She put the glass down. "This is the hardest part."

There was more?

"Are you familiar with the Kongelian mating ritual?"

"I've never mated a Kongelian, but I've heard it's a brutal affair."

She nodded. "The Krall's ritual is somewhat similar to that. Answering the summons is not the end of the story. You'll have to prove worthy by subduing me."

Jack chuckled. "Since you are not a Kongelian, that won't be much of a challenge. Not that I'm accepting. I'm just stating a fact."

"Don't let my looks fool you. I'm stronger than the average human female, and I've been training for years." She looked away and continued in a near whisper. "An honorable way out is to let me win. If I overpower you, then you are not a suitable mate for me."

Honorable. Right. As if losing to a female could be honorable. Even if Leia was as powerful as B'Kala, it would still sting to lose.

At this point, however, the summons hadn't been officially issued, and he could just tell her in so many words to forget about it. Naturally, he could come up with great excuses for why this wasn't possible and compliment her beauty and attractiveness to lessen the sting.

But the thing was, he didn't want to refuse her, and not only because she'd tugged at his heart with that sorrowful out she'd given him. Leia didn't want him to bow out. She wanted him to do his best to prove himself worthy.

Unexpectedly, Jack wanted to prove it too, just not in a physical challenge that involved wrestling her into submission.

On the other hand, if Leia was indeed as strong and as well-trained as she claimed, refusing her stank of sexism, especially since the intimacy of such a wrestling match was not a problem. It was part of the game.

Besides, issuing a challenge and expecting a male to prove his worthiness wasn't all that different from what human females did. Instead of a physical match that they were most likely to lose, human females invented mind games to test their males' worthiness.

In Jack's experience, passing those tests was much more difficult than a wrestling match with the toughest of male opponents. In fact, most human males failed miserably at the games females played with ease. Fortunately, passing a minimum threshold was usually enough.

Except, it didn't inspire much respect.

Jack had always hated those games even though he could maneuver the maze with the best of them, and at thirty-four, he felt like a jaded old man.

He was also quite sick of the holographic-deck make-believe beauties he bedded on the long space voyages. Crew members were forbidden to him, and shore excursions were too few and far apart to satisfy.

Perhaps marrying the princess wasn't such a bad idea after all?

The question was whether Leia could join him on the ship. Her mother was still relatively young and nowhere near retirement. Was Leia required to attend court? Or could she join him on his voyages?

The idea of having her with him was growing on Jack by the minute. He loved hanging out with his crew, but he craved the intimacy of a life partner, and he couldn't have asked for a better one than Leia. Not only was she a stunning beauty, but she was also intelligent, well-spoken, and assertive. Not to mention a bonafide princess.

Reaching across the table, he took her hand and smiled. "I'm honored and delighted to accept your summons, Princess Leia. But..."

## 19

# LEIA

*ere it goes.*

Now Jack was going to list all the reasons why he couldn't accept, letting her down as gently as he could but still breaking her heart.

Without internalizing it, for years Leia had clung to the idea of one day summoning Jack as a lifeboat. He was her ticket out of the stifling social structure of the Krall nobility, her one chance at true happiness.

"But I'm not willing to give up my post to become a political figure. This can work only if you can join me aboard my ship, and I have to assume that it depends on your duties as the crown princess."

Slumping into the chair in a most un-princess manner, Leia let out a breath. "Is that the only but, or are there more?"

"For now, that's the only one."

If only it were true. She was afraid to hope.

"At this point, my main duty as the crown princess is to find a mate and produce an heir. My mother can assign the few duties she's given me to someone else. Provided she is in good health, I have about twenty years before she is ready to retire. You might make Admiral by then."

He chuckled. "I doubt it. I'm a good captain, but much more is needed to become Admiral, which is more of a political post than military. I'm not the best politician, which is something you should be aware of if you expect me to become king one day." He shook his head. "My mother is going to faint when she hears that. She's obsessed with royalty."

It was the first time he'd mentioned his family.

"The British and ours are the only ones remaining."

He chuckled. "On Earth. There are plenty of monarchies on other planets. She books her vacations according to the palaces she wants to visit."

"Tell me about your family. If it's okay, that is. I don't want to pry."

It wasn't that she wanted to hear all about them right at that moment, there would be plenty of time to do so later, but the alternative was talking about the summons, which had exhausted her by now, or awkward silence, which was even worse.

"Forgive me for being pragmatic, but before we start chitchatting about this and that, I need to know what else is involved in this summons business, and where do we go from here. Do you announce it? Does your mother have to approve? How does it work?"

He was right. It was better to get all the details out of the way so he could make an informed decision. Dragging it out would only make her miserable.

"The summons is a private thing. I write it down and send it to you. Usually, it is done by a messenger, but since we are voyaging together, I'll just hand it to you. You read through it and either accept by signing your name or return it unsigned, which is considered a great insult."

"What does the summons say? Is it like a marriage contract?"

"It's more like a letter of intent. When you answer the summons, you agree to follow the steps outlined in it. In the old days, if the joining resulted in a pregnancy, the signed summons was used as proof of paternity. Now it's like an engagement. A step before a regular wedding ceremony."

"Provided I can wrestle you down to the mat, so to speak. Who is going to be the referee?"

Leia felt her cheeks heat up. Hopefully, he was just teasing her. "It's not a wrestling match in a gym, and there is no referee."

"What happens if someone lies?"

That was inconceivable. "My people have many faults, but lack of honor is not one of them. My word and yours will do."

## 2 0

# JACK

"Okay, so how is it going to go down. You hand me the summons, I sign it, and then what?"

Leia's dark complexion turned so red she looked almost purple. "We retire to my quarters."

"And then what?"

She cleared her throat and looked away. "You said that you are familiar with the Kongelian mating ritual. It's very similar. You go on the offense, and I defend myself."

As the implications sunk in, Jack's enthusiasm evaporated in a puff of putrid smoke. What he'd imagined was a wrestling match, not an attack. "This is not going to work. I'm not a rapist."

"It's not like that. I'll go on the offense too. It's a game." She blushed even deeper. "If you wish, I can give you a holographic vid to watch. I think it will answer all your questions."

He arched a brow. "Krall pornography?"

"Educational material."

"Well then, why don't we watch it together?"

It was fascinating to watch her face change hues once again, only now the color drained away, leaving her skin looking grayish.

"I'd rather not. It's too embarrassing."

"If we are to become a couple, embarrassment has no place between us. Did you watch it?"

"Of course. How else would I know what to do?"

He leaned forward. "Did it arouse you?"

"Yes," she said in a whisper.

He pushed to his feet and offered her a hand up. "Let's go to your quarters and get that vid. I just hope I can still reserve one of the holographic chambers for us tonight."

"Tonight?" Leia squeaked.

"Are you losing your nerve, Princess?"

"No, of course not. It's just that I haven't drafted the summons yet, and things might get out of hand..."

It was a good excuse, but he wasn't letting her off the hook so easily.

Leia had cast the net, caught her big fat fish, but it seemed that she hadn't thought beyond that point. Which was fine. She'd done her part, and now it was his turn to take over and lead the way.

Pulling her against his chest, he threaded his fingers through her long, lush hair and pulled her head back. "I wanted to do this since the first moment I saw you." He crushed his lips over hers.

At first, Leia gave token resistance, but when he held on tight, she melted into him, her tall body going soft against his until he was propping her weight with his arm around her middle.

When he finally let go of her lips, they remained parted.

Her eyes still closed, she murmured, "I've never been kissed before. I can't believe that I waited so long."

He couldn't either. Tradition or not, Leia should have at least stolen a few kisses. She was too honorable for her own good. "I'm going to make sure to catch you up on all that you've missed."

"I'll hold you to this promise."

"I'm good for it, and I'm also good for a retroactive summons. No one needs to know what happened first." He waggled his brows. "The summoning or the joining."

"You are naughty." She lifted her lips to his and kissed him softly. "But for once in my life, I want to be naughty too. With you."

"That's my girl."

# 21

# LEIA

*T*he holographic chamber back home wasn't nearly as sophisticated as the one aboard Jack's ship, and the experience of watching the vid this time was startlingly different, especially after Jack had superimposed it on another program. In this modified version, they were standing at a window and watching the other couple in a building across the alley.

Leia had watched the same vid a thousand times, pleasuring herself while imagining that she was the woman engaged in the rough play with the handsome male. The couple wasn't real, but the generated images were near perfect. Live pornography had been outlawed centuries ago, and all that remained were these masterful simulations that looked real enough to fool the senses, especially when watched from a distance.

She was just getting into it when Jack halted the play. "I think I've seen enough," he said as he offered her a hand up.

That wasn't a good sign. "Did it repulse you?" She cringed in anticipation of his answer.

"Not at all. But I'd rather be doing than watching." He

tugged on her hand and brought her against his body. "My quarters or yours?"

"Yours." She didn't want to run the risk of one of her delegates deciding to pay her a visit.

"That's the right answer." He kissed her, his hands roaming over her back and inching toward her bottom.

She was supposed to give him a hard time, to struggle and scratch and hiss at him the way the female in the vid had done, but Leia just couldn't bring herself to do it. Not with Jack. She wanted him too much to even pretend to fight him off.

Letting go of her lips, he looked into her eyes. "I was expecting a vicious tigress, not a soft kitten. Don't get me wrong, I'm not complaining. I like you soft and sweet. But weren't you supposed to bite and scratch me like that female in the vid?"

"I was. I just don't feel like doing it. My predatory Krall instincts are apparently nonexistent."

"Hmm. I have an idea about how to kick them into gear." He tugged on her hand. "Follow me."

"Where are you taking me?"

"Just the control panel. Are you familiar with obstacle courses?"

"I have one at home."

"The one I have programmed is like nothing you've seen before. It's a simulation of the one in the academy, only tougher."

She arched a brow. "Are we going to compete?"

"We are going to play a game. I'll give you a one-minute head start, and then I'm going to chase you. When I catch you, you are going to concede defeat and surrender to me."

"That's perfect. It fulfills all the requirements without me having to actually fight you. You are a genius!" She kissed his cheek.

Looking smug, he wrapped his arm around her middle. "No, sweetheart, you are the genius for choosing to summon such a clever mate."

# 22

# JACK

*A*fter Jack had chosen the preferred settings for the game he wanted to play, he watched with fascination as Leia stripped out of her ceremonial robes, shedding layer after layer until all that was left on her tall, athletic body were a pair of black boy shorts and a matching sports bra.

If not for the tiny fangs making an appearance whenever she smiled, she would have looked like any other human woman her age.

Only more beautiful than most.

"You are gorgeous." He reached for her arm and rubbed his palm over the smooth skin. "And much slimmer without all those acres of fabric."

She looked down at her body. "Am I too skinny?"

"You are perfect. Ready to race?"

She looked him up and down. "Aren't you going to change into something more comfortable as well?"

In honor of the delegation, Jack was wearing his formal dress uniform, but he wasn't about to strip Tarzan style, chasing his Jane in his underwear.

Instead, he shrugged off his jacket, kicked off his shoes, and took off his socks. The obstacle course required the kind of acrobatics that necessitated the use of toes.

"You have nice feet," Leia said. "When we are alone together in our quarters, I want you to always walk barefoot."

They hadn't mated yet, and she was already getting bossy with him. Not that he minded. Jack appreciated a woman who knew what she wanted and wasn't shy about asking for it.

Leia fit the bill and then some. Jack hadn't expected his future wife to be the one doing the proposing, and he certainly hadn't expected to say yes.

And yet, here he was.

"Aren't you putting the cart in front of the horse? I have to catch you first."

She grinned. "I know you will."

"Don't make it easy for me. I'm looking forward to a challenging chase."

"Oh, don't worry about that. I'm going to give you a chase to remember." She winked. "Start counting."

He could've asked the computer to sound the countdown, but it was more fun to pretend the jungle was real and not computer generated.

The moment he said one, Leia sprinted ahead, caught a hanging rope, and swung herself up onto a bridge, then kept running.

He'd expected her to be good, but not that good. She was much faster and nimbler than he'd anticipated, and Jack realized that a minute was too long of a head start.

It was too late to change the rules at this point in the game, though.

Forcing himself to pace his counting, Jack sprang into action the moment he reached sixty. By then Leia had disappeared in the jungle, and unless she proceeded with utmost stealth, she was probably hiding somewhere.

Having the home advantage and endless hours of practice

meant that Jack could traverse the course with his eyes closed, but the place was huge and provided numerous hiding spots.

He could spend all night searching for his princess.

Over the next hour or so, Jack went through every hiding place he could think of, but he came up with a lot of nothing. She must have been moving from one spot to another without making a sound and without leaving a trace.

There had been no broken branches and no fallen leaves to indicate her passage.

When Leia had promised him a chase to remember, she hadn't been kidding. And she was good. While he couldn't see her changing positions, she obviously saw him.

A change of tactic was needed.

First of all, the white dress pants and the white T-shirt had to go. To make things more interesting, he'd chosen the night mode, and in the darkness, his clothes were the opposite of camouflage gear, giving him away.

It seemed that he was going to do this Tarzan style after all.

Ducking into a hiding spot, he took the garments off, folded them, and tucked them under a rock.

Clad in only a pair of black underwear, he crouched low and proceeded soundlessly toward the tallest tree in the obstacle course. He'd climbed it many times before, but that didn't make the task any easier. The sucker was smooth, and the distance between branches made it nearly impossible to climb, even for a tall guy like him.

And this time he would have to do it without breathing hard or grunting from the effort.

Well, he wanted a challenge, right?

# 23

## LEIA

*F*lattened on the ground, hidden by sparse shrubbery, Leia watched Jack approach the tallest tree in the obstacle course. Save for a pair of tight-fitting undershorts, his lean, muscular body was bare, and as he started climbing, performing the kind of acrobatics she would have never suspected an Interstellar ship's captain capable of, he was a sight to behold.

She'd seen the tree, even contemplated hiding in its canopy, but the smooth trunk was too thick for her to wrap her arms and legs around, and there was no other way to climb it. Or so she'd thought until Jack had proven her wrong.

A smile lifted one corner of her lips. She had chosen wisely. Jack excelled in everything he did, and she would have no trouble convincing the queen that he was a most worthy mate for her. But was he going to find her without her having to give him a clue?

She'd promised him not to, but he'd passed right next to her on his way to the tree without noticing a thing. The shrubs weren't dense and didn't look like a good hiding place, which was precisely why she'd chosen them. No one would think to take another look at them when there were so many better hiding spots.

People saw what they expected to see and ignored what they did not. It had been proven by countless experiments.

Jack was climbing the tree either to get a better vantage point, or to look for her in the canopy, but he wasn't going to see her from the top unless she attracted his attention by moving.

It wasn't easy to stay motionless. Small rocks and twigs poked at her belly, and the rough shrubbery scraped her legs and arms. But she was well-trained and could endure hours of this.

Hopefully, it wouldn't take Jack that long to find her.

# JACK

*H*alfway up the tree, Jack paused to catch his breath. Resting on the first branch sturdy enough to support his weight, he looked down.

From this high up, he could scan roughly about one-third of the obstacle course. Starting at the entrance, he followed one possible path after the other and the areas near them.

If Leia wasn't hiding in any of the usual spots, she must be hiding in plain sight. What had he overlooked?

With her dark coloring, she could blend into the shadows, and there were plenty of shaded spots to choose from. It was a gutsy move, but then his princess was not lacking in that department, or any other for that matter.

So far, he hadn't discovered even one flaw.

How had he gotten so lucky?

But first, he had to catch her, and she wasn't making it easy on him, just as she had promised.

Ready to resume the climb, Jack stood on top of the branch and took one last look down, this time scanning the area nearest the tree.

Something about the shadows cast by the shrubbery didn't

seem right, and as he focused his eyes on the spot, a big smile spread over his face.

Such an incredibly clever woman. She was only partially hidden by the shrubs, but the shadows of nearby trees took care of the rest.

From the pathway, she was invisible. He'd passed right by her and hadn't noticed a thing. Forgivable for a civilian, but not for a trained soldier. If Leia were the enemy, he would have been dead.

Again, he counted himself blessed and more lucky than smart to be chosen by this incredible woman.

Using the branch to swing himself to the other side of the tree and out of her line of vision, he climbed several more feet before reversing direction and starting his stealthy descent.

Hopefully, she was focused on the upper part of the tree, expecting to see him going up, and not down. If he managed to circle around and surprise her, it would be game over. But if she spotted him before he reached her, she would sprint away, and he might not be able to catch her.

His woman was incredibly fast.

Back on the ground, he crouched low and proceeded slowly, placing his feet with extreme care and keeping his breathing shallow.

There was nothing he could do about his heartbeat, though, which sounded thunderous in his ears. The excitement of the imminent conquest was not only pumping him with adrenaline, but also making him hard.

His Tarzan attire was proving advantageous in more ways than one. The club he'd sprouted in his briefs would have been painfully uncomfortable if he were wearing slacks, and it would have made his stealth progress much more difficult.

Except, he wasn't as stealthy as he'd thought.

As soon as Jack got to the edge of the shrubbery, Leia leaped up and sprinted away, her long ponytail flying behind her.

"Oh, no, you don't." He bound after her, his hand going for that long hair.

He could've caught it but didn't. Yanking Leia back by her ponytail would have hurt, and that wasn't part of the game Jack was playing.

Instead, he forced his legs and arms to pump faster and tackled her from behind. With his arms wrapped around her, he twisted mid-fall, landing on his back with her clasped tightly against him.

Leia fought, trying to get free from his hold, but he'd expected it and held on tight. She was strong, stronger than many of the men he'd sparred with, but not enough to over-power him.

"Do you concede defeat?" He caught her earlobe between his teeth and held on.

She shivered. "Not yet."

He bit down lightly and pulled.

When Leia moaned softly, he let go. It wasn't much of a threat if she enjoyed it.

Pushing up to a sitting position, he wrestled her face down over his lap and yanked her shorts down. "How about now?"

"Not yet." She bucked up, almost succeeding to break his hold.

Taking a risk, he tightened one arm around her middle, caging her arms against her body, and freed his other one to deliver a hard smack to her upturned bottom.

"How about now?"

She snorted. "You must be joking. That was nothing."

Jack could've reminded Leia of their deal. She was supposed to concede defeat and surrender the moment he caught her, but this was much more fun.

Not holding anything back, Jack delivered five more quick smacks to her small, delectable bottom, and then rested his palm on those smooth cheeks.

Two things surprised him. First, even though he had never spanked a woman in his entire life, not even during holographic encounters, and had never felt the urge to, he was enjoying this way too much. Secondly, Leia wasn't struggling or attempting to get free. Could it be that she was enjoying this too?

He asked again. "Ready to surrender?"

"Not yet." Sounding breathy, she'd given him the answer, and it was a definite yes.

# LEIA

*a*s she lay draped over Jack's thighs, Leia told herself that this was a necessary part of the challenge. After all, the modified version that they had invented didn't fulfill the part of her fighting her mate and him subduing her. This was a suitable substitute.

Except, she'd given Jack only token resistance, and then when arousal spread through her like wildfire, the last thing she wanted to do was fight him.

Heck, maybe when she was queen, she should change the mating ritual to a chase followed by a spanking. This was much more fun than the original version, but that was only because it was Jack and not some snobby Krall male.

She would have fought any of them until they ran away bloodied and begging for mercy. Maybe that was why she'd trained so hard. Subconsciously, Leia had been preparing for the most important battle of her life.

The life she wanted to spend with just one human male.

By now Jack must have delivered at least twenty smacks, and her bottom was starting to smart, but since her arousal intensified in direct proportion to the sting, she didn't want him to stop.

Except, he did.

With the arm holding her down loosening its grip, he was allowing her to get free, but at the same time, his other hand smoothed down her heated bottom, inching toward her feminine center.

The message was clear. If she wanted to stop him, this was her chance, and he was waiting for her to decide.

Leia had no intentions of getting free or stopping Jack, but she appreciated him for not taking anything for granted. Not even at this point in the game.

When she remained motionless, her body soft and her muscles loose, he continued his trek until his fingers brushed over her swollen lower lips.

Leia groaned, her heartbeat going wild in anticipation of what he was going to do next.

Was he going to penetrate her with his finger?

She had played with sex toys and with her own fingers, but it wasn't the same as having Jack do it. Sex wasn't just about the body, it was even more so about the mind, and the added stimulation was explosive.

But then he did something totally unexpected. Withdrawing his fingers, he rested his palm on her bottom again and asked, "Are you ready to surrender now, kitten? If you do, you'll get more of what you crave."

*Sneaky man.*

She wanted more of those magic fingers. Heck, she wanted more of everything, and apparently the only way it was going to happen was if she surrendered.

Leia didn't need to debate long to arrive at a decision. "I do."

"Say the words, Princess."

"I concede defeat, and I surrender to you, oh mighty Jack."

That earned her a hard slap on her bottom. "I expect my mate to address me with respect."

"Yes, sir."

He rearranged her panties back in place and then lifted her, setting her down on his lap with his arms wrapped tightly around her. "I'm falling in love with you, Leia." He kissed the top of her head.

"Why do you sound sad when you say that?"

"I'm not sad. I'm elated and surprised. I never expected to fall so fast and so hard. But you are just perfect."

That was better.

Cupping the back of his neck, she lifted her lips to his and kissed him, using her fangs to nip at his tongue but careful not to draw blood. She wanted to but was afraid it would turn him off.

As the kiss heated up, his hands roamed over her body, touching her everywhere except where she wanted to be touched.

Pushing on his chest, she looked into his eyes. "I'm ready for more, Jack."

"Let's make ourselves more comfortable, shall we?" He winked and turned his head in the direction of the holographic chamber's control panel. "Alexis, change program to Kirk's number twenty-three."

"Yes, Captain."

The obstacle course disappeared, replaced by an opulent bedroom with a huge poster bed occupying its center.

As he lifted her up and walked over to the bed, Leia asked, "Did you name your ship's computer Alexis after the former Federation's president?"

He chuckled. "The ship came with the name. I'm not its first captain."

# 26

## JACK

*D*espite how far he'd advanced in such a short time, Jack hadn't been first in anything significant. He hadn't been his parents' first child, he hadn't finished first in class in the academy, and he hadn't been this ship's first captain.

But he was going to be Leia's first, and it filled him with a sense of wonder and discovery more thrilling than his first voyage to the stars.

As he laid her down on the bed, he removed her hairtie and then gazed at her beautiful face framed by the long swaths of black silk.

"Stunning," he murmured. "A goddess worthy of worship."

Leia smiled shyly. "I have enough trouble with the princess title. A goddess is certainly too much."

He lay next to her and gathered her into his arms. "You are a princess to everyone else but a goddess to me."

"I can live with that." She snorted and quickly covered her mouth with her hand. "I'm sorry."

"What's so funny?"

She shook her head.

It was probably nerves. Leia was anxious about her first time with a man, and the truth was that Jack was nervous too. He'd never been with a virgin, and he wanted to make it good for her, which meant being extra gentle and going slow.

Softly stroking her back, he leaned closer. "Come on. You can tell me."

Pressing her nose to his chest, she giggled. "I just thought that you have a strange way of showing devotion to your goddess. I've never heard of spanking as a form of worship."

He chuckled. "My goddess is special. She enjoys this particular form of devotion, and I enjoy offering it to her."

She lifted her head and looked into his eyes. "Did you ever do this with anyone else?"

"No. You are the only one."

"I'm glad to have this first."

"I've never been in love either. You are the only woman I've ever loved and ever will."

Her smile turned into a frown. "You haven't known me for long enough to fall in love with me."

"Perhaps. But this is how I feel right now, and I don't think it's going to change."

He didn't expect Leia to tell him that she loved him too, not yet. But he knew that she did. His princess just needed more time to realize that.

"I love you too," she surprised him. "I've been in love with you for ten years."

He cupped her bottom and gave it a squeeze. "That doesn't count. You were a girl with a crush. Now you are a woman. My woman." He took her mouth in a hard kiss, ending the conversation for now.

As their tongues dueled, Leia nipped at his every chance she got, the little stings sending bolts of fire straight to his groin. His princess was part kitten and part tigress, and he loved both sides of her.

When she got carried away and bit down too hard, drawing blood, he slapped her bottom, not because he was upset, but because it was a good excuse and he knew it turned her on.

To prove it, she bit down again and sucked, making little mewing noises of pleasure as he kept smacking her ass. He wondered what she enjoyed more, the taste of his blood or his palm making contact with her bottom.

When he stopped, she licked the spot she'd bitten. It tingled for a couple of moments, and then there was no trace of her ever nicking it. His tongue was as good as new.

He felt like returning the favor, but since his saliva didn't contain healing agents, he decided to kiss the little hurts away.

Flipping her on her stomach, he pulled her panties down and went to work, kissing every inch of her gorgeous ass.

She giggled into the mattress, but as he dipped lower and kissed her labia, the giggles turned into moans.

# LEIA

*I*ndescribable pleasure.

Leia just wished she could watch Jack and see the expression on his face as he kissed and licked like a man possessed. Was he really enjoying this so much?

From what her friends had told her, and what she'd read, men did this out of obligation, usually returning a favor for oral pleasuring they'd received. But that didn't seem to be the case with Jack.

He was literally eating her up.

She should have been embarrassed by the slurping noises he was making, not getting even more turned on, but as Leia was discovering, she had a kinky side.

How wonderful.

Even a princess needed to be naughty from time to time, and what better way to let her bad girl out than with her man in their mated bed?

As he penetrated her with his tongue, thinking became impossible, and all she could do was focus on the feel of his hands on her ass, holding her gyrating hips from bucking off the bed, his warm breath on her wet folds, the shallow penetration of his tongue.

And then his finger replaced his tongue, slipping deep inside her.

As her hips surged up, he barely managed to hold on to her, rewarding her with a hard slap to her bottom and then a soft kiss to sooth the sting away.

Killer combination. At this rate, she was going to climax in no time.

"I want to see the expression on your face when you come." He gripped her hips and flipped her onto her back, then glanced at the sports bra she was still wearing and frowned. "This has to go."

Happy to oblige, Leia gripped the bottom edge, yanked it over her head, and tossed it to the floor.

Jack's mesmerizing blue eyes shone as he looked at her breasts, and under that intense gaze, her straining nipples got even harder.

"I have to kiss them." He climbed on top of her, caging her between his knees and dipped his head to take one stiff peak into his mouth.

A new rush of wetness coated her inner thighs, and seeking relief, she clumped them together.

Done with one nipple, he moved to the other, licking and nipping until she pushed his head away. "It's too much."

He pressed a soft kiss to one and then the other. "I'll give your sweet berries a short reprieve while I finish what I've started." He slid down her body and parted her legs with his hands.

Watching her face, he slipped a finger inside her, then lowered his head and flicked her swollen clit with just the tip of his tongue.

Once, twice, three times.

He then wedged a second finger inside her and closed his

lips over that most sensitive bundle of nerves. As a new rush of wetness coated his pumping digits, he slipped a third one, stretching her even wider.

Uncomfortable at first, her sheath soon got accustomed to the penetration, and Leia wondered whether he could fit a fourth one.

But he didn't. Instead, he curled them lightly, pressing against an ultra-sensitive spot on her inner wall. It was almost enough to send her catapulting over the edge, and when he sucked on her clit, the tether snapped, and Leia threw her head back as she flew apart.

Still reeling from the powerful orgasm, she felt Jack climb back up on top of her and position himself at her entrance.

Lifting her arms, she clutched his shoulders, waiting anxiously for the hard plunge that was sure to hurt despite how well he'd prepared her.

"Don't be afraid," he whispered in her ear. "I'm going to be gentle."

For some reason, she was reminded of the time she'd dislocated her shoulder. The doctor had said something similar, and she'd believed him, but he'd lied. Snapping that shoulder back in place had hurt like hell.

But this was Jack, and she trusted him even though she barely knew him.

"I'm not afraid."

Gripping himself, he brushed his shaft over her wetness, coating it in her juices and brushing against her clit. Over and over again, until she was panting in anticipation.

"Please, Jack. I'm ready."

She expected a hard plunge, but Jack was as good as his word, pushing just the tip in, then pulling back, rocking himself gently into her in tiny increments.

It cost him.

His jaw clenched and his brows furrowed, he was dripping sweat as if he'd just finished back to back marathons.

She loved him for this, for putting her needs first, for giving instead of taking.

She couldn't have chosen a better mate.

And then he was all the way in, filling her, stretching her impossibly wide, but there was no pain, just an incredible feeling of fullness, of togetherness.

Her heart swelling with emotion, she wrapped her arms around his muscled back and held on tight. "I love you, Jack."

He lifted his head and looked into her eyes. "I love you too."

Slowly, he pulled almost all the way back, then surged all the way in, and as she moaned, he did it again, faster this time.

Heat washing over her, Leia held on tight as Jack let loose and pounded into her, not sparing her anything. When she exploded once again, he threw his head back and roared his climax, his essence pouring into her.

## JACK

*M*ind blowing, exhilarating, it was the best sex of Jack's life.

As an overwhelming feeling of love and gratitude washed over him, it eclipsed even the postcoital bliss.

Dropping to his side, he took Leia with him, not willing to withdraw or let go of her yet. Or ever. If he could have his way, they would stay in this bed forever.

Shifting in his arms, Leia nuzzled his neck. "Can we sleep in here?"

He groaned. "I'm afraid not. The session will time out soon."

"Then let's go to your quarters and sleep there." She lifted her eyes to him. "If that's okay."

It killed him to hear her say it.

"I don't need a piece of paper to make you my wife. From now on, you sleep nowhere else but in my bed."

"We need to make things official first. I don't want anyone contesting our union on a technicality."

Leia was right. He could see Meroll using every legal loophole to make their union impossible.

Jack had seen the way the bastard had been looking at Leia

when he thought no one saw him. He assumed she was his for the taking.

"We will do it first thing in the morning."

Reluctantly, Jack pulled out, grimacing when Leia winced. "Are you sore?"

She chuckled. "Of course, I am. It would be insulting to you if I weren't."

"Nonsense. I don't want you hurting because of me."

She smiled and kissed his cheek. "That's so sweet of you, especially since you enjoy spanking me so much."

"That's different. It's for our mutual pleasure."

"So is this. I'm sure next time I won't be sore. And besides, a soak in a bathtub should take care of that."

"Wait here." Jack got up and collected their clothes off the floor.

He handed her his T-shirt. "You can use it to clean up until we get to my quarters."

"Thanks."

Shrugging his uniform jacket over his bare chest, he buttoned it all the way to the top. If they bumped into anyone on their way to his quarters, he didn't want to give anyone material for gossip.

A ship was like a village, and gossip spread lightning fast.

When Leia was dressed, he took her hand and held his communicator in the other, checking the hallways for crew members. "I'll try to get us to my quarters without running into anyone."

They made it without incident, laughing as they stripped out of their garments and rushed into the bathroom.

After filling the tub for Leia, Jack stepped into the shower for a quick wash before slipping in behind her.

"How is the soreness, better?"

"Much." She leaned her head on his chest. "This is nice. I like being with you."

He nuzzled her neck. "I'm so grateful for your gutsy initiative. I shudder to think that without it I would have remained a miserable bachelor, not knowing what I was missing."

Leia sighed. "It's easy to get used to good things and then wonder how you could have lived without them. As much as I fantasized about you during the past ten years, I could not have imagined this closeness. You were an idea in my mind, an icon. The real you is so much more than that."

He caressed her long hair. "I'm glad I didn't disappoint you."

She turned around in his arms and kissed him. "You've exceeded all of my expectations."

# 29

# ALICIA

"Time to wake up, Alicia."

*Who's Alicia?*

Leia remembered falling asleep cradled in Jack's arms. Was this a dream?

"Alicia, open your eyes, dear."

Groggy, she did as the woman asked, blinking as the bright light shone into her eyes.

She was in a room full of equipment, but the light didn't come from a fixture. Warm sunshine was pouring from the open window, and puffy white clouds dotted the pale blue sky.

This wasn't an Interstellar ship, cruising in the inkiness of space, and she wasn't Princess Leia of the Krall. She was Alicia Fraser, a Starbucks barista during the day and a singer at night.

Captain Jacques Kirk wasn't her fiancé. His real name was Gregg, and he was nothing more than a virtual hookup.

It had been one hell of a ride, though.

"How are you feeling? Still disoriented?" The technician asked.

"No, I'm fine. The first moments were tough, though. I thought I was still my fantasy avatar."

The technician started removing the sticky pads. "Did you have a good time?"

"It was great." Alicia chuckled. "You were right. It's hard to get back to reality. I can see how this can become addictive."

"I get it a lot. Most people want to stay in the fantasy world."

Like Jack. Correction, like Gregg.

Was she sure it had been Gregg, though?

Yeah, she was.

He'd changed his eye color, but other than that his Avatar looked a lot like him. Then again, when asked to describe her ideal partner, she'd described Gregg, so the avatar could have been matched to that.

It had been such a strange fantasy. It had all the elements she'd requested, but there had been so much more. People with great imaginations must have created stories that could be adapted to fit various fantasies, like a different species occupying the Arctic circle, vampire-like beautiful creatures with fangs who at one time had subsisted on human blood.

The virginity hadn't been her idea either.

Who wanted to be a virgin in their fantasy?

But it had worked out fine. She had fun.

The most surprising part was the commitment. She hadn't requested it as part of her fantasy, and yet Gregg had not only played along, but had seemed to genuinely want to marry the princess.

Maybe there was still hope for him?

# 30

# GREGG

*T*hat had been the weirdest fantasy Gregg had ever taken part in.

And the most satisfying.

In fact, he'd been disappointed when he woke up and realized that it hadn't been real. Was his subconscious trying to tell him that it was time to settle down?

Gregg enjoyed his carefree bachelor life, but what he'd said as Jack was true. He hadn't known what he'd been missing until living the part of Captain Jacques Kirk and agreeing to wed Princess Leia of the Krall.

What a trip.

He'd gone down the rabbit hole enough times to go through most of the basic scenarios the programmers of Perfect Match had designed as the basis for the various fantasies people came up with. But it had been his first time with the Krall element.

Compared to the more mundane billionaire, pirate, mobster, rock star, or even alien invader scenarios, this one was pretty 'out there.' He would have to ask Gabriel who'd programmed that one. He or she deserved an award.

What Gregg knew for sure was that he wanted to go back and keep playing with Alicia. He wasn't ready to commit in the real world, but he could try it out for size in the virtual one.

# 31

# ALICIA

"You've been acting strange lately." Marcy gave Alicia a once over. "And you've lost weight. Gaunt is not a good look on you."

"I know. I'm so busy and running around so much that I don't have time to eat."

"Then slow down. Who is chasing you?"

Alicia grimaced. "No one. Just my demons."

A month had passed since her first virtual encounter with Gregg, aka Captain Jack. There had been many more since. When she'd gotten home that first day, an email was waiting in her inbox, requesting another virtual appointment, all expenses paid.

She'd accepted because she could not bring herself to refuse. In the fantasy world, Alicia had been the happiest she'd ever been, and it was impossible to give that life up.

Leia and Jack had arrived on the Krall home planet, established an embassy, and had left Meroll there as the Earth Krall liaison. On the way back, they'd had a wedding onboard Jack's ship with her mother's blessing.

They were the ideal couple, leading an ideal life, and like an addict, Alicia kept coming back for more. Except, upon waking up at the end of the sessions, she was feeling more and more depressed because her real life sucked. Gregg no longer came to her Starbucks for coffee, and their only contact was in the virtual world, playing make believe.

She had to stop that and start living for real.

Spending three hours twice or thrice a week in the Perfect Match studios was taking time away from her music career, and Alicia had no intentions of spending the rest of her life working as a barista.

That was why she'd declined the last invitation and then spent the rest of the day crying, mourning the loss of an imaginary relationship.

# 32

# GREGG

*S*am walked into Gregg's office, plopped a Starbucks coffee cup on his desk, pulled out a chair, and sat down. "Talk to me."

"About what?"

"About what is eating you lately. I miss my laidback chill partner. It's my job to be grumpy and demanding. Your job is the be the nice guy everyone turns to when they are pissed at me."

Reaching for the cup, Gregg shrugged. "Withdrawal is a bitch."

"Is that what it's about? You are trying to quit caffeine?"

"Very funny, Sam. It's not about coffee. It's about the virtual reality thing. I'm done with that."

Sam nodded. "Good for you. It's about time you started living in the real world. What happened, a bad experience?"

"Just the opposite. It was too good, and then she quit on me, and I can't play with anyone else."

Arching a brow, Sam crossed his legs. "I thought the allure was the choice of partners. You want to tell me that all this time you were playing with only one?"

"Just for the past month." Gregg grimaced. "Best fucking month of my goddamned life."

A big grin spread over Sam's face. "Congratulations, buddy. You found your perfect match. Just ask for a face to face with her. I only hope she is as good as her avatar."

"She is."

"You've met her?"

"You've met her too. Alicia, the Starbucks barista."

"The one with the tattoos?"

Gregg nodded. "Now you know why I can't be with her in real life. Can you imagine me bringing her home to my mother? She would drop dead on the spot. Besides, I don't know if Alicia is still interested in me. She declined my last invitation."

"So, she knows who you are too?"

Gregg nodded again.

"I don't want to know how you pulled that off. I hope you didn't hack into Perfect Match's servers because that would be a serious violation."

"The only thing I did was to check when her application was submitted. It's not a big deal."

"Even that was illegal and an invasion of her privacy, but it's not like I'm going to report you."

"Thank you."

Sam rubbed his hand over the back of his neck. "Your mother will not drop dead because of a few tattoos, and you know that. It's just an excuse. If you tell her ahead of time, maybe even show her Alicia's picture, she would be fine. Alicia is beautiful, and she seems like a nice person. I'm sure your mother can overlook superficial things like body decorations she's not fond of."

"I don't know if Alicia even wants to see me."

"Then find out. Go to that damn Starbucks and talk to her."

Gregg shook his head. "It's not that simple. We got married

in the virtual world. She wouldn't accept anything less in the real one, and I'm not marriage material."

"For a smart man, you are incredibly dumb. You've just told me that the month you've spent with her was the best one of your life, and that if you can't play with her you don't want to play with anyone else. It's a no brainer, Gregg. Marry the girl and live happily ever after in this world, not in the fantasy one."

# ALICIA

*S*omething was up. Marcy was smiling all through the shift, and she wasn't the only one. Alicia's other coworkers were also casting her amused glances when they thought she wasn't looking at them.

It wasn't her birthday, so it wasn't a surprise party. Was she getting a promotion? Or maybe the Bravo award?

That must be it.

Nice. She'd been busting her butt for a long time in this branch and deserved some recognition.

"Alicia," her manager called. "Can you give me a hand? The delivery truck is outside, but his dolly has a busted wheel, and he needs us to help him carry the boxes in."

"Sure." Alicia stifled a smile.

It was a ruse to get her out for a few minutes so they could pull out the banner or whatever else they'd prepared for the occasion.

Playing along, she followed Tiffany out back. "Where is he?"

"He's coming." Tiffany was doing her best to keep a straight face and failing.

When a stretch limousine pulled up to the curb, Alicia

108

thought nothing of it. Sometimes the flower shop next door decorated them for weddings.

Except, the limo stopped right in front of her, and as the passenger door opened, Gregg stepped out, wearing a suit and looking like the rich guy he was.

"Hello, Princess." He took her hand and lifted it to his lips for a kiss.

Stunned speechless, she just stared at him.

"Congratulations," Tiffany whispered before ducking back inside and leaving Alicia alone with Gregg.

What the hell was she talking about? Congratulations for what?

The mystery was solved when Gregg dropped to one knee and pulled out a small box from his pocket. "Will you marry me, Alicia? Say yes because I can't live without you. Well, I can, but it's a shitty, lonely life, and I want to have my happily ever after with you." He flipped the box open, revealing a huge diamond ring.

*The nerve of the guy.*

Alicia pulled her hand out of his grasp and crossed her arms over her chest. "The best I can do is maybe."

She should have known that he wouldn't be easily deterred.

Still down on one knee, he looked up at her with a cocky smile on his handsome face. "What will turn it into a yes?"

"Time. We need to get to know each other first."

"We already do. Come on, Alicia, I know that some groveling is required as penance for my stupidity, but you and I know that we are meant for each other. Say yes, and I will spend the rest of my life making you happy."

Behind her, the door opened, and Marcy stepped out. "Say yes, or I will. A hunk with a limo and a diamond ring is too good to pass up."

There was much more to Gregg than that, but if he was even half as good as Jack, then he was a keeper.

Gregg was Jack, though, and the only reason to refuse him would be petty vengeance for making her miserable when she'd thought it was over between them.

"Yes."

Gregg blinked, once, twice, then a huge grin spread over his face, and he leaped, lifting her in his arms and twirling her around.

"She said yes," Marcy shouted, and a moment later the rest of her coworkers spilled out the back door, clapping and cheering as Gregg kept twirling her around.

Her head was spinning by the time he stopped and crushed her to his chest. "I promise you that you are never going to regret it. You've just made me the happiest man alive."

# EPILOGUE

"Grandma, when is mommy going to sing?"

"When the warmup band is done, sweetie."

Gregg's mom kissed the top of his daughter's head.

Sitting in his mother's lap, Riley turned around and cupped her cheek. "How much longer?"

"Not long."

"Daddy?"

"Yes, sweetheart."

"I'm tired."

"Do you want to sit on me?"

"Yes, please."

Gregg lifted his little girl off his mother's lap and cradled her in his arms. "Close your eyes. I'll wake you up when mommy goes on."

"Okay."

As he held her close, her soft hair tickling his chin, Gregg's heart swelled with love. The past five years had been the happiest of his life, and he was looking forward to many more.

"I'm so excited for Alicia," his mother said. "This is the biggest crowd she's ever performed for. I'm proud of her. It

111

isn't easy balancing motherhood with a singing career." She patted his arm. "You are a good husband, Gregg. She couldn't have done it without you."

"And you." He leaned and kissed his mother's cheek. "If you didn't volunteer to babysit Riley every time we needed it, it would have been much more difficult for us."

She waved a dismissive hand. "Riley is the joy of my life. You couldn't keep me away even if you wanted to."

Thinking back to his unfounded fears about his mother not accepting Alicia, Gregg shook his head. He hadn't given his mother enough credit. She'd hated the tattoos, but she'd fallen in love with Alicia.

Life was good and getting even better.

His mother didn't know it yet, but in seven months, their little family was going to welcome another bundle of joy.

Dear reader,

Thank you for reading Perfect Match 3: Captain's Conquest. As an independent author, I rely on your support to spread the word. If you enjoyed the story, I would be grateful if you could post a brief review on Amazon.

Kind words will be greatly appreciated and get good Karma sent your way -:)

**Click here to leave a review**

Love & happy reading,

Isabell

---

## THE CHILDREN OF THE GODS
### DARK STRANGER THE DREAM

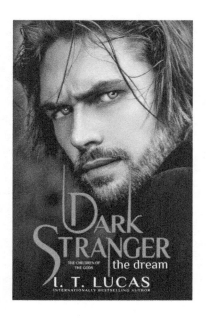

# FOR EXCLUSIVE PEEKS AT UPCOMING RELEASES & A FREE COMPANION BOOK

JOIN MY *VIP CLUB* AND GAIN ACCESS TO THE VIP PORTAL AT
ITLUCAS.COM

CLICK HERE TO JOIN
(http://eepurl.com/blMTpD)

### INCLUDED IN YOUR FREE MEMBERSHIP:

- **FREE CHILDREN OF THE GODS COMPANION BOOK 1** (INCLUDES PART ONE OF GODDESS'S CHOICE.)
- **FREE NARRATION OF GODDESS'S CHOICE—BOOK 1 IN THE CHILDREN OF THE GODS ORIGINS SERIES.**
- **PREVIEW CHAPTERS OF UPCOMING RELEASES.**
- **AND OTHER EXCLUSIVE CONTENT OFFERED ONLY TO MY VIPs.**

**If you're already a subscriber, you'll receive a download link for my next book's preview chapters in the new release announcement email.** If you are not getting my emails, your provider is sending them to your junk folder, and you are missing out on **important updates, side characters' portraits, additional content, and other goodies.** To fix that, add isabell@itlucas.com to your email contacts or your email VIP list.

**NOTE FROM THE AUTHOR:**

**PERFECT MATCH 3: CAPTAIN'S CONQUEST
is a work of fiction!**

Names, characters, places and incidents are products of the author's
imagination or are used fictitiously and are not to be construed as real. Any
similarity to actual persons, organizations and/or events is purely coincidental.

Made in United States
North Haven, CT
06 December 2023

45175741R00068